Falling in Like

Melissa.J.Morgan

First published in the UK in 2008 by Usborne Publishing Ltd., Usborne
House, 83-85 Saffron Hill, London EC1N 8RT, England. www.usborne.com

Copyright © Grosset & Dunlap.
Published by arrangement with Penguin Young Readers Group, a division of
Penguin Group (USA) Inc. of 345 Hudson Street, New York, NY 10014,
USA. All rights reserved.

Cover photography © moodboard / SuperStock

The name Usborne and the devices ♀ ⊕ are Trade Marks of Usborne
Publishing Ltd.

A CIP catalogue record for this book is available from the British Library.

ISBN 9780746093429   JFMAMJJASON /07   Printed in Great Britain.

PROLOGUE

Posted by: Val
Subject: Candy War! & TRAUMARAMA!

Happy November, ladies of the Camp Lakeview 4A/4C Bunk Alliance! As your official blog "Scream Queen", I'm checkin' in to say I hope you all had a fab Halloween. I'm so glad we are still staying in touch. Thank you to our counsellors, Becky and Andie, for setting up this two-bunk blog for us!

Okay, here are the results of our trick-or-treat contest:

A big sugar high-five for Jenna! She won with 178 pieces, and that's not counting the sixteen booger-flavoured Bertie Botts that her twin bro Adam snuck into her sack. Chelsea was a close second with 152. Grlz, you totally put the "puke" in Camp Lakepuke!

Now for Best Costume:

The winner is...Brynn, the White Witch of Narnia. She got "lucky thirteen" e-votes. As you can see from her pic, she looks...chilly!

So, do you guys want to do anything "together" for Thanksgiving?

On to my TRAUMA: Last Friday my Aunt Juanita had back surgery, so my mom flew to Maryland to take care of her for a few weeks. This means I have to stay full time with my dad, my stepmom Sharin, and my stepsister LaToya. As if that weren't bad enough...our brand-new low-flow toilet overflowed...and guess whose room it flowed into!

SO...I'm bunkin' with LT until my room is fixed. She has gone completely kookoo over my "invasion" of her "personal space". She says it isn't "fair" and I agree. I think it would be more fair if every shoe she owned got soaked with pee water! (J/K)

I hope you ALL will write lots of posts and e-mail/IM me so I can "retain a pleasant attitude" (my mom's words) until my mom comes home. I am trying really hard to roll with this but I'm pretty sure I'll need some support from my CLFs (Camp Lakeview Friends).

So, what's up with everyone else? I know you're all busy but we want to know what you're busy with!

KIT,

Val

CHAPTER ONE

Alyssa sat at a computer in her middle school's media centre and read Val's blog post. Poor Val was having a pretty tough time with her stepsister. Val didn't even like hanging around LaToya at her dad's house on weekends. Now she was stuck there 24/7 until her mom came home.

Alyssa wanted to write Valerie back right away to show her support, but the study hall bell was due to ring and she didn't want to be late for her art class. Today they were going to sketch an actual artist's model, and Alyssa could hardly wait!

I'll write Val tonight from home, Alyssa decided. With a glance at the clock above the mega-colourful mural of pioneer life, she powered the PC down. Then three...two...one! The bell trilled, signalling the end of the period.

Grabbing up her backpack and her charcoal-coloured puffy down jacket, Alyssa left the media centre. Her beaded chandelier earrings tickled her jaw line as she joined the chattering throngs of students in the main hall. She had "artist" written all over her look – along with the paint-flecked black T, she also wore a black jeans skirt, black boots and a cool black knitted cap she had found in her mother's old packed-away clothes. Her fingers sported cranberry-red polish, and her matching lipgloss was a total score from her favourite ninety-nine cent store.

Other kids rushing to their next-period classes surrounded Alyssa. Up ahead, Beckah and Rose, her art class BFFs, zoomed into the art room. Alyssa dodged around a group of boys and dashed in after them.

As she crossed the threshold, she skidded to a halt. *Wow.*

A statuesque young woman was perched on a stool next to Mr. Prescott's wreckage of a desk. She was dressed in monochromatic indigo – a navy blue boatneck sweater and a pair of dark blue jeans – and her profile was very distinct – high forehead, ski-slope nose, a little overbite and a pronounced jawline. Her neck was as long as a giraffe's, practically. Alyssa assumed she was their model. All in all she was an art student's dream model, dramatic and exotic-looking.

Sweet!

Alyssa entered her sanctuary. The art room was her favourite place in the entire world. The walls were covered with student artwork, intermingled with prints by some of the greats – Degas, Cezanne, O'Keeffe, and the *Tar Beach* illustrations of Faith Ringgold. She inhaled the scent of creativity – a mixture of oil crayons, chalk, oil paints and clay dust. She said her hellos to Beckah and Rose as she took her chair across from them. The three buds were clustered in the middle of a big, long table they shared with seven other students.

There were a total of twenty-five students in the class. Everyone was pulling out their sketchpads and making a big deal out of selecting which pencil to use, even though they were all standard-issue No. 2s. Some of the boys were snickering as they glanced at the model, and Alyssa just rolled her eyes. Middle-school boys were *so* immature.

"This is going to be cool!" she said to the girls, pulling a ginormous rubber eraser from her heavily-stickered purple plastic art box and setting it next to her pencil. Mr. Prescott, her art teacher, liked to say that there were no mistakes in art. Maybe not, but there certainly were do-overs.

Beckah nodded excitedly. "I can't imagine posing in front of a roomful of people. I'm going to feel weird staring at her," Rose whispered.

"She's a *model*," Alyssa argued. "She's used to it."

"I would hate it," Rose insisted.

"That's why you're *not* a model," Beckah said.

The bell rang, and Mr. Prescott bustled in from the hall, balancing a stack of long, flat boxes of oil pastels and a stack of papers against his chest. His goatee, heavy eyebrows and buzz cut floated above his tower like a caricature drawn on a balloon.

"Good morning, *mes artistes*," he said, as he plopped everything down on his very messy desk. Alyssa wondered if it was true that there was an entire three-year-old pizza on the bottom layer of sketches, canvases, memos, posable wooden figurines, unopened paint cans and art books. That was the rumour.

"This is Willa Ackel, our model for this morning." The model smiled at Mr. Prescott and then at the class. "We'll begin sketching in a moment, so Willa, you can hang out. But first, let me tell you artists about a contest you are all invited to enter."

Alyssa raised her brows as she smiled eagerly at Beckah and Rose. An art contest? Rock!

"Some of you have heard of *Works*, our school arts quarterly," Mr. Prescott continued. "The first issue for this academic year will be out in a couple of weeks."

Alyssa nodded. *Works* was a great journal. She had pored over the last year's issues. Some of the art was good enough to hang in galleries. And the poems and short stories were fantastic. She hadn't had the nerve to submit anything of her own. After all, she had been a brand new middle-schooler.

Mr. Prescott continued. "Last year, the editors kept getting submissions from the same few people over and over. So this year's staff decided to run a contest to encourage more people to contribute. The prize will be a showcase in the next issue. There will be five pages of art from the visual arts winner, and five pages of stories, essays, or poems from the language arts winner."

"Whoa," Beckah murmured. "That's seriously cool."

"There are a few rules," Mr. Prescott said, "and you can only submit one entry. The deadline is in two weeks. If you're interested, please pick up a flyer after class."

Interested? Who wouldn't be?

Across from Alyssa, Rose crossed her eyes and wrinkled her nose as if to say, *No way.* But Beckah mouthed at Alyssa, *I'm in!*

Alyssa whispered back, "Me, too!"

"All right, let's get to work," Mr. Prescott said, clapping his hands together. He smiled at Willa, who sat taller on her stool.

Alyssa settled in, raising her arm over the blank piece of paper. She glanced over at Willa, making mental notes about her proportions as she got ready to make the first, defining line.

But to her surprise – and that of everyone else in the class – Willa climbed on top of the stool, raised her hands high over her head, arched her back, and gazed up at the ceiling.

"Oh," Mr. Prescott said raising his bushy eyebrows. "Interesting choice."

I totally love it, Alyssa thought. It was a magical moment – Alyssa could actually see her finished sketch in her mind as she looked from the model to the blank page and back again. It was as if she were working *with* Willa, and together they would make every pencil mark on Alyssa's sketch paper.

I'm in the zone! Alyssa thought, and quickly went to work.

Priya and Jordan stood like prisoners in front of Ms. Romero's desk in the science lab. She had her grade book open, and there was bad news.

Priya and Jordan had C's in science. C's were not good enough for their two sets of parents. They *had* to raise their grades or they would be grounded for the rest of their natural lives.

"Here's what I suggest," Ms. Romero said. "The

Tri-County Regional Science Fair is six weeks away, and if you can put together projects good enough to enter into the fair, I'll give you twenty points of extra credit."

That would give me a B, Priya calculated, *and J a B-minus.*

"We're in," Priya said, speaking for both of them. Jordan nodded like a bobblehead.

"Totally in," Jordan agreed. He smiled at Priya. "We need a team name. We'll be the Titans of Science."

"How original," Priya said, laughing. Their school mascot was the Titan.

"Wait." Ms. Romero raised her red pencil in the air, signalling a flag on the play. "I know you two are best friends. Do you think you will distract each other if you team up together to work on this?"

Priya and Jordan shook their heads in unison. "No way!" Priya said. "We'll help each other. We live next door, so we can meet after school every day without worrying about transportation and things like that."

Jordan nodded. "We do tons of stuff together. We even planned our camp trip to Washington DC, together."

"On the other hand," Ms. Romero continued, cocking her head in that way she had when she was thinking through all the variables of an experiment, "maybe it would be better for each of you to team up with someone who is a little stronger in science."

Their faces fell. No Priya and Jordan? No Titans of Science?

"Please?" Jordan begged. "We'll do an awesome job."

"We totally will," Priya promised.

"All right," Ms. Romero said. "We'll give it a try. But I want to see your progress, all right? I want you to come up with your project idea and fill out a proposal packet by Friday. That gives you all week. I'll look at it over the weekend and let you know next Monday whether or not you can proceed."

She leaned forward as if to emphasize her next words. "You need my okay to enter the fair."

"We will amaze you," Jordan promised.

"Just do a good job," Ms. Romero said.

Yes! Priya grinned at Jordan. He grinned back. Now they were next-door neighbours, BFFs *and* fellow mad scientists.

"Here's the proposal packet." Ms. Romero pulled out a drawer and extracted a thick stack of stapled pages. "Remember, I need it Friday."

"Got it." Priya took the papers from her and unzipped her backpack. She carefully slipped the packet into a dark purple folder and rezipped her pack.

"Thank you so much, Ms. Romero," Priya said. "We won't let you down."

"That's good to hear," the teacher said as she closed the drawer, signalling that it was time for them to go.

They left the science lab together to go to their lockers before leaving. They always walked home together. They lived most of life together.

"So, we need a topic," Priya said.

"Gas is always good," Jordan replied. "How about 'What burns up more calories, burp gas or fart gas?' We could light our farts and our burps, and make a cool graph. You know science fair people are into graphs in an extreme way."

"You cannot light burps," Priya insisted.

"Oh yeah? Ever tried to?" Jordan asked, waggling his eyebrows. "Because we can go home, get some matches, and drink way too much root beer."

"You're on!" Priya cracked up. Jordan started laughing, too.

"Hi, guys," said a voice behind them. "What's so funny?"

It was Leslie Graff, the star of science class. Leslie wore her black hair pulled back in a ponytail and her glasses were so dirty, Priya couldn't figure out how she saw through them. It was like she couldn't even take the time to clean them, because she was too busy doing science experiments.

Leslie was very serious about school. She was so

smart that she had actually found an error in their science book and pointed it out to Ms. Romero. Her backpack was usually crammed full of library books and she always did all the extra credit. Priya figured she would eventually invent a time machine or something.

"We're discussing topics for our science fair project," Priya said, elbowing Jordan not to add any details. Priya was much better at being friends with girls since last summer at Camp Lakeview, and she knew they didn't usually joke with each other about burping and farting. She didn't want to gross Leslie out.

"That's always a difficult choice," Leslie said, nodding with a look of authority. Her face took on a dreamy, faraway look. "There are so many possibilities."

"Well, what's your topic?" Priya asked her.

Leslie's eyes gleamed. Then she narrowed them as if she were stalking a wild animal. "I have a couple of projects in mind, but I'm leaning towards photosynthesis," she declared with an air of mystery.

"Oh," Priya said, a little taken aback by her intensity. "Cool."

"Yes." Leslie paused. "I think I may have some competition, though. I believe Marco Rubio is also considering a plant experiment." Her cheeks turned a little red. Then she said, "Not to worry, though. I'll blow him out of the water."

Wow, she is really into this fair, Priya thought. Leslie certainly didn't need the extra-credit points, so she must have been in it for the glory.

"Plants are popular," Priya observed. Her girl-discussion skills were still kind of new, so she wasn't sure what else to say.

"Marco's always on top of the trends in science," Leslie went on, and her cheeks turned a little redder. She blinked and cleared her throat. "Well, I'm going to the library to do some more preliminary research. See you guys tomorrow."

She gave them a little wave and walked on.

"Isn't photosynthesis kind of over?" Jordan asked Priya.

"Not if the two biggest science geeks in our class are into it," Priya observed. "And I mean 'geek' in the good sense," she added, because she liked Leslie and she didn't want Jordan to think she was being snarky. "Maybe we should do photosynthesis, too."

Jordan did a theatrical double take and gaped slack-jawed at her. "Are you nuts? Those guys will blow *us* out of the water. There's no way one science fair can handle *three* photosynthesis projects. We *have* to get into the fair to get the extra credit. We have to think of something different. Unique. Unusual. Something that's never been done before."

He had a point. Priya started mulling.

"But on to serious stuff," Jordan said as they swerved around some band kids carrying large instrument cases. "Brynn's birthday is in three weeks!"

Priya rolled her eyes. "That's more serious than our science fair project?"

"No, but it's fairly urgent," he replied, as they reached his locker. He twirled the combination lock with a deft, practised hand. "Round and round she goes, to ten, twenty-two and lucky thirteen!" he cried.

The locker swung open. On the interior of the door, Priya saw the six pictures of Brynn at camp, which Jordan had made into a collage, plus the cover of the programme of the play he had seen with Brynn in DC.

"So, what kind of stuff does she like?" he asked Priya.

"Fake vomit is always nice," Priya replied helpfully. "Hey, we could do our project on the chemical components of vomit."

"That sounds like a possibility." He reached into his locker, came out with a gooey half-eaten apple in his hand, and winced. They weren't supposed to keep food in their lockers. Especially rotting food.

"What's her favourite colour?" he asked her.

"Of vomit?" Priya asked. "Jordan, focus." She gave his arm a little sock. "Science fair."

"Science fair. I'm good. I'm in the game," he promised her, rummaging around and finding a wadded-up paper bag. He dropped the apple into it. "What about a gift card?"

It went like that for the entire walk home. Jordan turned every single one of Priya's attempts to talk about their science project into something about Brynn's birthday present. By the time they reached their block, Jordan had thought up and discarded at least a dozen gift ideas.

How many science fair project ideas had he come up with?

Zero.

"Want to shoot some hoops?" Jordan asked. "Let's play horse."

"Okay. Tell you what," she said. "Whoever loses has to fill out the proposal packet."

"You're on," Jordan said.

Jordan took off his backpack while Priya retrieved her basketball from the big bin o' balls in the garage.

She tossed the ball to him and he dribbled it the length of the driveway, whistling to himself as she shadowed him.

"Check it out," Jordan crowed as he laid up the shot.

Just before he let go of the ball, Priya said, "She might like a charm bracelet."

He jerked around. "What?"

The ball rebounded off the rim and bounced onto the cement. "No fair!" he cried, catching it. "You distracted me!" He gave the ball a few more dribbles and threw it at her. "Charm bracelet? You think?"

Priya smiled to herself as she caught the ball. She was onto something here. Two more distracting gift suggestions, and there would be no proposal packet in her future.

"Maybe," she said, squinting past the ball to the hoop. She eyeballed her trajectory. Jordan was shifting his weight from foot to foot like he was going to steal the ball from her any second.

"But if I were you..." she ducked around him and lofted the ball into the air.

Slam-dunk! It plunked right into the basket.

"Lucky shot," Jordan sniffed. "If you were me, what?"

She gestured to the basket. "Take your best shot, Jordan." She waited while he shifted his weight, eye on the hoop. He licked his lips, going all intense, and she attacked, getting right in his face as he worked to keep the ball from her. He was taller, but she used that to her advantage, to grab the ball when he was dribbling it.

"If you were me, what?" he asked.

She pivoted and took off. He chased after her, all arms and legs and Jordan. He scooped the ball away from her and got ready to throw.

Then, just as the ball was about to leave his hands, she said, "Hair scrunchies."

His throw went wild. "Oh, that's not fair!" he cried.

She laughed and did a victory dance.

"Sorry," she said, all innocence. She could see that he was mentally filing the suggestion away for further consideration, like Leslie Graff and her big treasure trove of science project possibilities.

"Where do you buy them?" Jordan asked.

Priya won the game – no surprise – extracted Jordan's blood oath that he would, indeed, fill out every single blank in the proposal packet, then clean forgot to give it to him before she went into her house to start all her other homework. No biggie. She'd get it to him in *plenty* of time to fill it out.

CHAPTER TWO

"Valerie!" LaToya snapped as she tapped her extra-long French-manicured nails against the grey metal locker next to her stepsister's. Her heavily made-up face was scrunched up in total scowl mode. "The last bell of the day rang about a year ago! They are *waiting*. Let's *go!*"

Valerie clenched her teeth to avoid a sharp retort. Her mother had asked her to get along with her stepsister while she was with Aunt Juanita, and she would – even if it killed her.

And it just might. I. Am. Going. To. Explode!

She grabbed up the books she needed for her homework, stuffed them into her backpack, and trailed in LaToya's wake of perfume and attitude as they headed out the main entrance of Marie Curie Middle School.

Valerie's parents had been divorced for a long time. Her father had married LaToya's mother two years ago, and the two stepsisters went to the same middle school. They were only eleven months apart in age, but they were in different grades and hung out with totally different people. LaToya's crowd was noisy and dramatic, mostly cheerleaders and dancers, like her. Valerie's friends were a little more down to earth.

Make that *a lot* more down to earth.

LaToya was dressed in scarlet, from her wool trousers to her sweater to her winter coat to her earrings, lipstick and the beads in her cornrows. Valerie felt kind of washed out in black and grey, even though her friend Shaneece had told her she looked totally fab and "very sophisticated".

When her mom was in town, she picked Valerie up after school. But her mom wasn't there. So after some discussion, her father and stepmother had concluded that she would have to come home via LaToya's carpool — except LaToya's carpool didn't take LaToya home. It took her to Fusion Space, the dance studio where she practically lived, and LaToya's mom picked her up from there on her way home from work. Valerie would have to go there, too. Every day after school.

So her father had come up with a "great" idea this morning during the drive to school: *Valerie* could take classes at Fusion Space, too!

"Daddy, please, no," Valerie had begged, glancing at

LaToya in the rear-view mirror of their black Camry. Her stepsister was seething, and Valerie got why: Fusion Space was *her* thing. LT had been going there for six years and she was the total queen of the scene. She didn't want to share her bedroom *and* her dance studio with Valerie.

But as her dad pulled to the kerb to let them out, he said, "You used to love your ballet classes. Just try it, okay?"

Valerie would rather do extra homework in every subject ever invented than have to deal with an added daily dose of her stepsister's attitude. But she had said, "Okay, Daddy," because she had promised her mother she'd get along.

Her father had called her on her cellphone at lunch to tell her it was all arranged. The school director herself would evaluate Valerie for placement during LaToya's class. As her father had pointed out, Valerie had taken a lot of ballet in elementary school and she had totally loved it. Once she got to middle school, she kind of just stopped going. So she wasn't too nervous about having to audition. She knew she was a good dancer.

But she also knew that LaToya would resent her invasion of more of her "personal space". Sure enough, LaToya had been snotty to her all day, and Valerie was dreading being in class with her.

"See? The van is practically about to leave," LaToya said, turning around to glare at her.

Along with a winding parade of SUVs and minivans, a white Odyssey was crawling towards the pick-up location next to the school's flagpole. It was up next – which was a far cry from "about to leave".

"Toy-toy!" Danielle Wilcox cried as she threw back the sliding door of the van. Then Danielle muttered, with a distinct lack of enthusiasm, "Oh, yeah, Valerie, too. I forgot you'd be here today."

"Hello, Valerie. I'm Danielle's mother," said the driver of the van. "I don't think we've met." She was a pleasant-looking woman in workout clothes, with her brown hair sheared into an athletic-looking cut.

"Nice to meet you, Mrs. Wilcox," Valerie said.

"Toy, listen! I have such good gossip!" Danielle announced, scooting over so LaToya could sit next to her. LaToya plopped down and pointedly set her backpack on the seat beside her, so that there was no room for Valerie.

Valerie glanced at the three-person seat behind LaToya and Danielle. Maryann Killeen and Emily Jones – the two other carpool girls – were already arranged with all their stuff in the places closest to the door and the middle. The space furthest from the door was loaded with their backpacks. In other words, there was no room for Valerie to sit there, either.

"C'mon, girls, make some room!" Mrs. Wilcox urged them as the car behind her beeped its horn.

Maryann rolled her eyes and picked up first one backpack and then the other, as if they each weighed a million kilos. She plopped one of the backpacks into Emily's lap. Then she shuffled on her bottom *verrry slooowly* towards the window. Emily scooched into the middle as if the effort was sapping her last bit of strength. Valerie squeezed herself into the vacated space, wedging her fat backpack on the floor beside the door.

"Thanks," she said.

"No problem," Emily grunted.

"Punch it, Mom!" Danielle said as LaToya pulled the van door shut.

The Odyssey wove back into the traffic. LaToya and Danielle yakked and giggled, mostly about boys. Emily and Maryann chimed in now and then when the topic switched to other girlfriends they had in common. Danielle's mom turned on the radio to a station LaToya requested, and soon the heavy bass beat of hip-hop surged through the floor. But Valerie wasn't feeling the music. She wasn't feeling anything but lonely and left out.

* * *

27

Fusion Space was in a funky part of Lennox, Pennsylvania, near the local university. The dance studio sat in the centre of a busy, artsy block. There were eateries serving Ethiopian, Indian and Thai food; a used record and DVD shop; and a goth store called Cemeteria that featured black T-shirts and plush vampire bat stuffies in the window.

As Mrs. Wilcox pulled up to the kerb, LaToya slid back the door and gathered up her stuff. "You need to call me later let's *go* Valerie," she said to Danielle, all in one sentence, as if Valerie had been holding them up again.

Then LaToya jumped out and headed for the purple studio door without waiting for Valerie.

"Thanks for the ride," Valerie said to Mrs. Wilcox, who smiled and gave her a jaunty wave.

Valerie caught the door as it swung behind LaToya. FUSION SPACE was written across it in green and black letters. Below it were the studio's hours, and then DANCE written sideways. It looked very cool.

Just beyond the door, a cute guy with green eyes and dreadlocks sat at an ebony desk. Framed photos of dancers in striking deep-hued robes and large African-style headdresses lined the back wall. He was talking into a headset, but Valerie had no idea how he could hear anything, because loud, pulsating music was blaring from the back of the building.

"Hey, Antoine," LaToya said, as she picked up a pen and checked off her name on a printed list labelled "Advanced Interpretive Movement". She had to work at it because of her long nails. LaToya was in all the advanced classes at the studio, rising through the ranks with years and years of study. She also assisted with the beginners' classes to help with her tuition. Before that, she had helped with the phones herself.

"My stepsister," she said as she finished signing in. She put down the pen. She jerked her head at Valerie. "C'mon."

Still on his call, Antoine fanned his fingers at Valerie as she hurried past him to keep up with LaToya. The two girls zoomed down a narrow hall lined with more photos and a poster of a dancer who was apparently named Alvin Ailey.

LaToya parked herself in front of a door marked "Ladies' Dressing Room", wrapped her hand around the knob, and glared at Valerie.

"I have to change," she announced. "Go see if they have practice clothes to lend you."

She opened the door, and noise poured out – chatting, laughing girls, slamming metal locker doors. Someone called, "Toy!" LaToya darted in and shut the door in Valerie's face.

O-kay, Valerie thought, her face burning. *Not wanted in the dressing room.*

But she did need to score some clothes to wear. She thought about asking Antoine for some, but he was a guy and she felt funny. So she kept going down the hall. The music grew even louder, and Valerie realized she was bobbing her head to the rhythm. It was very cool, very tribal, and her shoulders were moving, too.

There was a green and purple beaded curtain at the end of the hall. She walked through the curtain and into another world – a world that took her breath away.

Reflected in mirrors that spanned the back of the room, three dancers were dressed in black leotards and tights, wearing black and gold masks that looked like fierce jungle cats. LaToya had told Valerie that Fusion Space had a professional company that performed throughout Pennsylvania. These must have been some of those dancers.

They were leaping and pouncing in a circle as a tall, barefoot woman in a black leotard and a shiny black floor-length wrap-around skirt watched from the sidelines. She was beating out the time on the wood floor with a long stick. Her black hair was plaited into a dozen braids dotted with silver beads, then twisted and held in place with two beaded picks. She had on heavy eye make-up and dark red lipstick.

Sprawled on the floor along the front of the room, eight or so girls about Valerie's age were dressed in black, green, fuchsia and purple leotards and footless tights of all sorts of colours, some with their hair pulled back, others opting to let it hang loose over their shoulders. One lay with her head on the floor, her legs stretched open in an incredible side split. Another sat cross-legged, leaning over a book. She had a pink highlighter in her right hand. Two other girls were making hand motions that mimicked those of the three dancers, as if they were the learning the dance's steps. Another was texting into a BlackBerry.

"Strong arms! Think about your power!" the woman encouraged the dancers, keeping time with her stick.

As the music swirled and rose, the dancers leaped into the air with their knees pulled underneath them, then fell to the ground, rolled over, and pushed up on their hands, arching their backs. Then they did body waves as they got back up, posing with their fingers curled like claws. Drums thundered and they flew around the room, faster and faster, leaping higher and higher, until the music stopped with a clash of cymbals and a tinkling of bells.

The dancers froze in three different positions, one on her back with her leg up high over her head, one dipping towards the floor with her leg extended behind her back, and the third with her arms reaching straight towards the ceiling. It was a very stunning finish.

"Wow!" Valerie blurted into the silence.

The three panting dancers, the girls on the floor and the woman all turned to look at her. Someone giggled.

She flushed bright red. "Sorry," she murmured.

The woman grinned and cocked her head, gesturing with her stick to indicate that the performers were dismissed. As they sidled away, she said to Valerie, "I appreciate your enthusiasm. Are you the new student?"

"Oh, no, I'm LaToya's stepsister. I mean, yes. I guess I am," Valerie said, tongue-tied.

The woman looked Valerie over. What did she see? Too tall? Too short? Dancer-like? Not dancer-like?

"Your father mentioned that you need some clothes. I think we have something that will fit you," she said. "Do you have a sports bra?"

"Um," Valerie managed, flushing harder. "No. Not with me. I didn't know I'd be dancing today."

"No problem," the woman assured her. "We'll get you ready. I'm Manzuma, the director," she said. "I own the studio."

Valerie gulped. *Way to make a good first impression.* This was the woman who was going to watch her in class. LaToya called her "strict" and "demanding". She said sometimes some of the students would cry in class because

Manzuma worked them so hard. She forced them to do the same moves over and over until they dropped.

"Nice to meet you," Valerie said in a small voice.

"You're not nervous, are you?" Manzuma asked, narrowing her eyes in mock-suspicion. "Dancing is hard work, but it's also fun."

The woman led Valerie back towards the beaded curtain just as LaToya and two other girls passed through it. LaToya was dressed in a scarlet leotard and matching tights, and her hair was pulled back with a beaded red scrunchie. The other girls were just as colour-coordinated, one in black, and one in China blue. They looked like real, professional dancers.

LaToya smirked at Valerie. "Yeah, Val, get ready to have some *fun*."

"Oh, I *am* ready," Valerie said. It came out much cockier than she had intended, which was unfortunate. LaToya would definitely make her pay for that.

"We'll see," LaToya said, as she danced a bunch of very fancy steps over to the ballet barre bolted to the wall. *Very* fancy.

Payback time!

This is really working, Alyssa thought excitedly as she added a scarlet wash to her portrait of Willa Ackel. She was working in her studio. Or rather, the corner of her bedroom that she'd turned into a studio with the help of her father.

Alyssa was covered with cyan and indigo. Her fingertips were smudged with Indian ink. She had used a calligraphy pen to write a poem she had entitled "Ode to a Woman" around the silhouette.

I
am
I am a
woman-to-be
a woman-to-be strong and free
I am
a body humming
a heart strumming
a spirit thrumming
changing, growing, becoming,
I
I am
I am a
woman now
I!

Yes! It perfectly described how she felt about growing up.

Alyssa had drawn Willa so that it was hard to make out her sweater and blue jeans, and she wondered if she should emphasize the texture of the sweater a little more. Otherwise, Willa looked kind of...naked.

I don't want to mess it up, Alyssa thought.

She straightened her back and rolled her neck. Then she stood back, still unable to believe that she had actually created this masterpiece.

Now she had just one problem: which of her thousands of paintings, drawings and sketches should she select for her five pages in the *Works* showcase?

Dressed in black tights that barely covered her knees and an olive-coloured leotard silk-screened with a turquoise dancing koala bear, Valerie stumbled *again* as LaToya's entire Advanced Interpretive Movement class leaped like gazelles across the floor. Valerie's legs weighed six hundred pounds each as she tried to copy the lithe movements of the well-trained dancers.

Humiliated, she stared down at her feet. Her toenails looked awful. It was autumn; who bothered with pedicures when everyone wore close-toed shoes?

Modern dancers, that was who. Unlike ballet dancers, who wore slippers, Manzuma's students went barefoot. Everyone else's toes were filed and painted, and one girl had glued little rows of rhinestones along the cuticle lines of her two big toes.

And no one else was wearing a hideous olive-and-turquoise-dancing-koala-bear leotard. In fact, none of them had dancing animals of any kind slapped over their chests.

But those were only the minor details that made Valerie wish there was a trapdoor she could fall through. They couldn't come anywhere near her complete and total mortification: she was blowing her placement audition. She, who had taken ballet for years, was so nervous, she was jerking around like a string puppet.

As a ballet dancer, she was used to a whole different set of steps, and turning her legs and feet outwards. But in this class, everyone kept their legs and toes pointed forward. Apparently this was more "natural" than ballet. But it didn't feel natural to her. She kept forgetting and trying to do things ballet-style, and then she would mess up and trip again. It was awful.

"Okay, for the last five minutes of class, I want everyone to improvise," Manzuma announced, walking directly in front of Valerie. She crossed her arms over her chest. Her friendly smile had long ago frozen in place, as if she couldn't believe that someone related to LaToya was such a total klutz.

"Imagine that you're a Zulu warrior princess,"

Manzuma told Valerie. Her gaze swept over all the students. "You're fighting a lion!"

Valerie didn't know anything about Zulus. *I am Xena, Warrior Princess*, she thought, feeling too dejected to put much effort into her attempt. She tried to put on a fierce "grr" face and stab an invisible spear at an invisible lion. Her improvisation was completely lame. LaToya flew all over the room while Valerie pretty much stood in one place, jabbing her hands forward.

Maybe I should name my lion "LaToya".

"Love-ly," Manzuma said after, oh, five years. She clapped her hands. "Thank you, class. Valerie, stay with me, dear."

The other students strode across the dance floor, chatting about class and who got the showers first. LaToya glanced over her shoulder at Valerie, then left with her friends.

Once they were alone, Manzuma said, "I believe your father said on the phone that you've taken some dance before."

"Ballet," Valerie replied. "But I stopped a couple of years ago." She took a breath. "So maybe I'm a little rusty, but I'm sure I'll catch on quick."

"Modern dance is a very different animal from classical ballet," Manzuma said. "Sometimes it's hard to make the switch."

She's telling me I sucked. Mutely, Valerie nodded.

"That's all right. We can take care of that. In the beginners' class," Manzuma said kindly. "It starts in about ten minutes. How would that be?"

That would suck, too, Valerie thought. *Totally.*

"LaToya usually helps me with that class," Manzuma continued, "because her mother is still at work, and can't get here any sooner. So maybe you could do your homework or read a book during the advanced class, and then take the beginners' class."

Which LaToya helps with, Valerie thought miserably.

"Why don't you give it a try tonight?" Manzuma urged her. "We'll see how it goes. You're not too tired, are you?"

Valerie thought about her father. She thought about her mom and her plea to Valerie to maintain a pleasant attitude.

And then she sighed inwardly and said, "No, I'm not too tired."

To: Val
From: Alyssa
Subject: My art piece!!

Dear Val,
   I wanted to thank you for telling us that story

about Ugandan women singing to girls when they get their first periods. That was my inspiration for this piece I did tonight. I'm attaching a jpeg for you. I am calling it Ode to a Woman. I think the woman looks like she is dancing my poem!

XO,

Lyss

To: Alyssa
From: Val
Subject: Your art piece

Dear Lyss,

Your picture is so beautiful! I wish I could dance like that. I did terrible in LT's class and now I have to take the beginners' class. I was really bummed but your pic helped cheer me up.

Your friend,

Val

CHAPTER THREE

Posted by: Alyssa
Subject: Rejected!

Hi, everyone,

Happy Tuesday...not!

Yesterday we had a model (for the first time ever!) and she looked so strong and proud while she was posing that I got totally inspired. First I sketched her in pencil and then I did a wash, and added some oils...anyway, that's technical artist talk.

I was inspired to write a poem around her silhouette about becoming a woman. I remembered Val's story about Ugandan women singing to girls when they start their periods. You can see it pretty well in the pic I attached. I didn't say anything about getting your first period or *anything* like that. I stayed up all night working on it. (And I am way busted because I didn't do the homework for any of my other classes.)

But this afternoon when I handed it in to Mr. Prescott, my art teacher, he said it was "inappropriate" and he wouldn't let me enter it into the contest! I am really bummed out!

I don't understand why he won't let me use this picture. It is my BEST ever! I hope you will tell me what you think. Be HONEST. If you think Mr. Prescott is right, tell me!

TTFN,

Lyss

Posted by: Sarah
Subject: Your Picture

Dear Lyss,

Abby and I think your art piece totally rocks. It reminds us both of a soccer jock. Maybe Mr. Prescott will change his mind.

Your friend,

Sarah (and Abby says hi!)

PS: Abby sent the jpeg to her cousin. She's in design school in Rhode Island.

"Check it out, Kallista. I brought us yummy sushi," Tori announced as she unpacked their lunch at an outside table in the landscaped area at Beverly Hills Middle School. It was Tuesday, very sunny and warm, and Tori and her best friend, Kallista Goldman, were wearing frilly tops and knee-length skirts. November in Southern California could go in either direction — from blazing hot to foggy and chilly. Today was a picture-perfect let's-get-a-tan-at-lunch kind of day.

Kallista laughed. "Tori, you have brought sushi for your last three turns."

They always took turns bringing lunch for each other, getting their moms or dads to buy delicious

42

takeout-y things during their shopping trips to one of the several gourmet grocery stores near their houses in Beverly Hills. Today was Japanese – California rolls and *ebi*, which was cooked shrimp on squares of rice. Yesterday Kallista had brought Thai.

Kallista slipped off her lacy sweater and put it over the back of her beige metal chair while Tori opened the drawers of the little lacquered Japanese bento box she had packed their lunch in. The box was a gift from supermodel Astrid Landon, who had bought it on her recent Tokyo photo shoot. Tori and Kallista both knew Astrid. Kallista's father was a director who had cast her in a few movies of his, and she was a client of Tori's father, who represented all kinds of Hollywood actors, producers and directors.

"I was reading my two-bunk blog in study hall," Tori told Kallista. She brushed a few tendrils of blond hair out of her eyes and took apart her wooden chopsticks. "My friend Alyssa is really upset. She made this incredible painting for a contest, but her art teacher won't let her enter it. And she stayed up all night working on it!"

"That stinks," Kallista said as she reached over and dipped a piece of California roll in a tiny black lacquer dish of soy sauce mixed with a dash of wasabi. "Isn't there anyone else Alyssa can talk to?"

"Her art teacher is in charge of the contest," Tori said. She nibbled on a piece of *ebi*. "I guess what he says goes."

"That's censorship," Kallista stated with an air of authority.

"What's censorship?" asked a voice. And not just any voice. *The* voice.

Tori's mouth went suddenly dry. Somehow, she managed to turn her head.

Against the soundtrack of her thundering heartbeat, the new guy, Michael Stevenson, stood between her and the sun. His curly golden blond hair glowed like a halo. His deep blue eyes sparkled like the waters off Malibu. The freckles across his nose were adorable. And could she *be* any more in total crush mode?

She had been crushing on him ever since school started. The weird thing was, she hadn't told anyone about it, not even Kallista. Maybe because this felt like a *real* crush, and not the silly semi-pretend crushes they had each had in the past – like on movie stars and older boys. Michael was a guy their age, and it was kind of embarrassing to admit that she like-liked him.

It was just so extremely cliché. Michael was the hottie *every* girl was crushing on. He had just transferred from a school in Glendale. His father, the actor Cameron Stevenson, was the new big thing – as big as

Natalie Goode's father, in fact, and that was saying something. So the Stevensons had moved from their little bungalow in Glendale to a big Beverly Hills mansion, smack in the middle of Tori's school district, her zip code, and her heart. It was November and she had been into him since September...three months of butterflies every time he talked to her. It was getting really hard to act normal around him.

"Hey, Michael," Kallista said in a friendly, offhand way.

"Hi." He smiled at Kallista and then his eyes just sort of bored in on Tori like laser beams...or so it felt to her. Suddenly all her thoughts were beginning to...dissolve.

"Would you like some California roll?" Kallista asked him.

"Thanks. Sure," Michael said.

Tori was wistful. Why hadn't *she* thought of offering him some sushi?

Michael bent down as Kallista offered him a morsel of California roll. Tori stared at his perfect lips while Kallista continued to carry the rest of the interaction. "Tori's got this friend who tried to enter an art contest at her school. And some teacher said she couldn't, because her sketch was 'inappropriate'." She made air quotes.

Michael chewed thoughtfully. Then he swallowed and said, "Like how?"

Kallista looked at Tori. She knew that was her cue to make her mouth open and words come out. The English language. She used to be good friends with it.

"She sent us all a pic of it," Tori said. "It's beautiful."

"Well, what did he say was wrong with it?" Michael persisted.

"He only said it was inappropriate," Tori said. "It's of this model."

Michael considered. Then he turned a little pink. "Well, is she, um..." He trailed off and looked down at his feet.

Oh, no way, Tori thought. Her face went hot. *He thinks she's naked!*

"No, no," she said quickly, shaking her head so hard the tendrils of hair fell into her eyes again. "She's wearing clothes, they're just coloured in lightly. That's why it's so unfair."

"Maybe the teacher wants someone else to win," Kallista ventured. "So he wants to lock out the serious competition."

"That's so Hollywood," Michael drawled, grinning crookedly. "I don't think things like that happen in..." He looked at Tori. "Where is this?"

I can't believe it! We're talking to each other. We're having a conversation. This totally rocks.

"Alyssa lives in New Jersey," Tori said. She was

46

beginning to recover from the shock of his arrival and move into actually enjoying his presence. "And I don't know if you're right about the competition, but I do know that teacher is wrong. It's *beyond* beautiful. It should win!"

Michael raised a brow. "Not if she can't even enter it. The teacher has the final say."

"But what about free speech?" Tori argued.

"Yeah," Kallista said. "What about that?"

The five-minute warning bell sounded. Michael said, "Well, I guess we'll have to continue this later."

Yes! Yes! Yes! Tori thought, but she said as casually as she could manage, "Okay. Sounds great."

Michael gave them both a friendly wave and moved off. Kids in shades started packing up their lunch stuff.

"Why didn't you tell me you're crushing on him?" Kallista asked Tori after Michael left.

Tori grimaced and smiled at the same time. "Was I that obvious?"

Kallista laughed and pulled out her cellphone. She put it to her ear without pressing any buttons and said perkily, "Hello, is this Whole Foods grocery store? We'd like you to cater a wedding!"

"Oh, shut up!" Tori cried, and the two girls burst into laughter.

* * *

After school, Tori and Kallista had a tennis lesson with Suki Schroder, the tennis pro at their swim and racquet club. Tori's mom met them there to watch and played doubles with them for a little bit. Her mom was tall and willowy, and since she was the beauty editor for an online magazine, she always got samples of the newest make-up. It was very cool.

Tori and Kallista told her about Alyssa's dilemma and Tori's mom said, "Sometimes the artistic road is a bumpy one."

Then Tori's mom had to leave for a meeting with some cosmetics people, and Kallista was scheduled for a maths tutoring session. Blair, Tori's father's assistant, picked Tori up and dropped her off at Sitar, where her dad was having dinner with a new client. He had invited Tori to join them.

"My client has a son about your age," her father had told her. "You two can talk while we discuss business."

As Tori swept through the restaurant, she spotted her father at "his" table – the one with the best view of the waterfall and the live peacocks – and waved at him.

Then her jaw dropped as she saw who was sitting with him. Cameron Stevenson.

And Michael was with him.

Michael is the "son about my age"! I'm having dinner with Michael!

Jangly nerves warred with chilly thrills at the very thought. She wanted to jump up and down and pass out at the exact same time.

"I *neeeeed* you, Kal-lis-ta," she sang to herself, wondering if it would be rude to hang a U, go into the bathroom, and call her friend for moral support.

Then she bagged that thought, because Michael had risen from the table and was actually walking across the restaurant towards her! He had this great quirky half-grin and *ohmigosh*, could he be *any* cuter?

"Hi," he said. "I guess it's *later* now."

She stared at him.

"Remember, at lunch?" he said. "When I said maybe we could talk about your friend, I had no idea it would be *later* so soon."

"My friend..." she said slowly. Her brain finally engaged. "Alyssa! Yes!"

"Are you okay?" he asked, peering at her with those Pacific Ocean eyes.

"Yeah. Fine," she croaked. As discreetly as she could, she cleared her throat. "So. My dad's a lawyer. We can ask him about Alyssa's free speech."

"Coolness," he said.

He turned and headed back to the table. Tori floated after him, about a metre off the ground.

* * *

On Wednesday afternoon, Priya and Jordan sat on their tall science lab stools as rain and thunder rattled the rafters. At the front of the lab, Ms. Romero was wearing science-y hot mitts and goggles as she held a test tube over a hissing Bunsen burner. The test tube was plugged with a stopper that had a thin tube running through it. Over that, a balloon was attached to the outside rim of the stopper.

Leslie Graff was sitting behind Priya. "The principle of hot air," she murmured.

Jordan grinned at Priya and mouthed, "Also known as *gas*."

The thunder rumbled again, and the lights in the science lab flickered. At the same time, the balloon inflated. A bunch of the students cheered and applauded.

"It's alive!" Jordan cried. "It's alive!"

"That's from *Frankenstein*," Priya said. "Boris Karloff. After the mad scientist zaps the monster with a gazillion watts of electricity."

"Yes. You get ten points!" Jordan informed her. They kept scores on movie trivia. They kept scores on everything.

"Of course I do," Priya crowed. "Let's go for fifty. Whoever gets fifty first, the other one has to type up our science fair report." She already had him on the proposal packet; why not go for the whole enchilada?

"I wonder if Brynn likes horror movies," Jordan said, his eyes going all soft-focus. "Maybe I could buy her a DVD of *Frankenstein* for her birthday."

"Jor-dan," Priya said. "Did you not hear me? Science fair report?"

"On farting," he said.

"We cannot do our report on farting," she retorted.

"Why not?"

She thought for a moment. Then she remembered the new entries she had read this morning on the Camp Lakeview blog site.

"It would be inappropriate," she informed him. "We would end up with D-minuses in science, or even worse."

"We should ask," Jordan said.

"We are not asking. Ms. Romero needs to know we are taking this seriously."

Jordan huffed and muttered, "Oh, all right. Fifty points. Movie trivia, horror, science fiction and fantasy."

"You're on." She grinned at him.

He smiled back and said, "So *do* you think she'd like a DVD of a horror movie for her birthday?"

"No clue," she replied.

Ms. Romero concluded her demonstration by letting all the air out of the balloon, with a distinctive fart sound. Jordan laid his head down on their lab table to stifle his laughter. Priya started cracking up, too. Then she remembered that Leslie was sitting behind her.

She turned around and rolled her eyes as if to say, *Boys are so immature.* But Leslie wasn't paying the slightest bit of attention to Jordan. She was gazing over at Marco Rubio with a little smile on her face.

Intrigued, Priya glanced at Marco. His eyes were glued to his notebook and he was taking notes as if his life depended on it. His eyes were kind of bulging beneath his extreme-retro black square glasses.

If Leslie had been trying to share the humour of fart noises with him, he was unaware of it.

Cradling his head in his arms, Jordan snorted. Priya gazed down at him and said, "Brynn would totally stop e-mailing you if she could see you right now."

"Would not," he said, but he looked the merest bit uncertain and sat up straight.

"May I see you two after class?" Ms. Romero asked them.

"Oh, great. Now you've gotten us in trouble," Priya said.

"*Me?*" Jordan whispered, all indignant. "You're the one who kept talking through the entire *fart* experiment!"

"Priya? Jordan?" Ms. Romero asked again.

"Yes, of course. After class. Check," Priya said.

The bell rang soon after that. As Priya and Jordan packed up their notebooks, Leslie said to Priya, "That was a neat experiment."

"Yeah." Priya ignored Jordan as he started snickering again.

"I once did a science fair project on anechoic chambers," Leslie continued as she started loading her science book into her backpack. How many books *were* there in there?

"How did you create the vacuum?" Marco Rubio

asked, walking up to them. He sounded like he was challenging her.

Leslie flushed, raised her chin, and said, "I used a generator."

"I didn't know they were allowed." Marco sounded suspicious.

"They were, back in my old school district," Leslie coolly informed him.

"Ah. I see." Marco adjusted his glasses. "I heard your new project is on photosynthesis."

Leslie shrugged. "Maybe."

"Prepare to be demolished, then." He smiled at her and headed out the door.

Jordan said to Priya, "Maybe *they* should get the T-shirts. Only theirs would say, 'Clash of the Titans of Science'."

"*Clash of the Titans*," Priya said. "Sir Laurence Olivier played Zeus."

"Who is Sir Laurence Olivier?" Leslie asked Priya.

"He's an actor," Priya told her. "Well, he was. He's dead."

"Oh." Leslie nodded. "Did you catch what Marco said to me?" She looked amused. "Of course I know we can't use generators."

"We're still, um, working our way through the proposal packet."

Leslie looked surprised. "Really? I turned mine in at the start of the semester."

"We just kind of recently found out about the fair," Priya said.

"Oh. Well, I keep up on science fairs," Leslie said. "There are all kinds of them, put on by lots of different organizations."

"Imagine," Jordan drawled.

"Yeah, well, see you." Then Leslie hoisted up her backpack and slid her arms through the straps. She gave Priya a little smile and left the lab.

"Were you making fun of her?" Priya asked Jordan.

"No. No way," Jordan assured her.

They walked up together to Ms. Romero's desk. She was putting away her science stuff.

"I wanted to ask you about your progress on your project selection," she said. "How is it going?"

"Uh, we're narrowing it down," Priya said, trying to sound more confident than she felt.

"We just found out, no generators," Jordan said sadly.

"But there are so many other topics to choose from," Priya added. "It's like this big buffet of science!"

"Well, I like that enthusiasm," Ms. Romero said, smiling at them both. "Don't forget that I need it by Friday."

"Not forgetting," Jordan said.

"In fact, we're going to go work on it right now," Priya assured her.

"Good," Ms. Romero said, placing her hot mitts in a plastic container labelled BALLOON EXPERIMENT. "That's the spirit."

They walked home. Jordan said, "I'll dump my books in my room and be right over."

"Okay." She didn't know why he didn't just bring his books, but it was no biggie either way.

"Hi, Mom," she called out as she went into her house.

Her short, dark-haired mother was in the kitchen, surrounded by large cardboard boxes on the counters and the floors. She looked a little overwhelmed. Make that a lot overwhelmed. Make that deer-in-the-headlights panicked.

"Some more supplies arrived," she told Priya. "There's so much to keep track of. I have a ton of invoices, too." The supplies were for Smoothie Town, Mrs. Shah's smoothie bar, which was scheduled to open at the mall that very week. She crossed her arms and gazed around at the disarray that used to be her kitchen. "I wonder if I ordered too many plastic cups?"

"I'm sure it's just the right amount," Priya told her, giving her a hug. She was so proud of her mom. "It's going to be great, Mom."

"Thanks." Mrs. Shah didn't sound convinced.

"Jordan's coming over," Priya said. "We're going to work on our science project."

"That's nice," her mom replied. "Maybe Jordan can help us load all this into the SUV." She made a face. "There's so much of it."

"You know he will."

Priya went into her room and slung her backpack onto her bed. After she powered up her PC, she took the folder containing the thick wad of science fair forms out of her pack and opened it. She read the first page, which contained a list of things they could not use in their experiment: "No live animals; no flames or fires; no noxious chemicals."

"Well, there goes our fart experiment," she said, grinning.

She sat down at her desk and kept reading. Marco was correct on the no-generators thing. She also found out that the top three winners of the Tri-County Regional fair would go on to compete in the state science fair.

There's no way we'd ever place first, second, or third, she thought. But that was okay. All they had to do was enter a project.

She was on the last page when it dawned on her that Jordan hadn't shown up yet. She looked at the digital time readout on her computer screen. Half an hour had passed since they'd come home from school.

Where is he?

On a hunch, she opened up her AIM box. Sure enough, there was his IM icon. And there was Brynn's — a girl inside a big glowing star.

<Pree>: Jordan? R u here?
<imnotmichaelJORDAN>: Yo!
<Pree>: JORDAN! U idiot! U r supposed to be HERE!
<imnotmichaelJORDAN>: OMG! Pri, I am SOOOOOO sorry!!!!!

Priya left his textbox unanswered as Brynn IM'd her.

<BrynnWins>: Hi, Priya!
<Pree>: Hi, Brynn!
<BrynnWins>: Guess what! I'm online w/ Jordan, too!
<Pree>: I know. He's supposed to be HERE, working on our science fair project.
<BrynnWins>: WHAT?!

"I hope she doesn't think I'm mad at *her*," Priya muttered.

She heard the phone ringing in the kitchen a couple of times. On the third ring, it was picked up.

Then her mother appeared in her doorway with the portable phone in her hand.

"It's Jordan," she told Priya. "I thought he was coming over."

"I don't want to speak to him," Priya said angrily.

On her screen, Jordan typed:

<imnotmichaelJORDAN>: PLEEZE talk to me!

Grumpily, Priya took the phone from her mother.

"You are so dead," she said into the phone.

"I know, I know, I suck," he replied, his voice filled with misery.

"You went home first to see if you had e-mail from Brynn, am I right?"

"Yeah, guilty as charged. I was just going to check quickly. I swear. I lost all track of time."

"That's not helping," she gritted.

"Oh, Pri, I'm sorry, I...it's just, she was online and I wanted to ask her what she wanted for her birthday and we just started talking and..." He trailed off. "Do you forgive me?"

"Sort of," she said. "Jordan, our topic is due on Friday and the form Ms. Romero wants us to fill out is a metre thick. You have *got* to come over here *right now*."

"Okay, right. I know. I'm on my way."

But fifteen minutes later...there was still no Jordan.

School for Wednesday was over, and so was Alyssa's life. Or at least that was how it felt, as she sat dejectedly in the art room with her *second* rejected submission for *Works*, her Impressionistic rendition of her mother's rose garden.

"It sucks," she muttered.

"No, it doesn't suck," Mr. Prescott assured her. He was sitting across from her at her art table, his hands folded as he regarded her watercolour. Upside down. *"Roses at Dawn* is very...nice. It just doesn't have the verve of your first piece. The energy."

"Then..." She took a deep breath. "Why can't I submit *Ode to a Woman*?"

He sighed and shook his head. "I'm sorry, Alyssa. It's just too controversial."

"But isn't art supposed to *be* controversial? Shake people up?" She was quoting one of his lectures, and she could tell he recognized it.

Before he could say anything, she added, "I can make her clothes more obvious."

He took a moment, looking down at all the light-speckled roses. "It's not that. I don't know how to explain this to you. *Ode to a Woman* is just...too mature for a middle school art show."

"It's R-rated?" she asked, trying to understand.

"More like PG-13," he replied.

"So we're back to *Roses at Dawn,*" she said.

"I won't forbid you from entering *Roses at Dawn* into the contest, but I have to tell you, I don't think it will win. It's just not your best work."

"Okay," Alyssa said, picking up her picture and inserting it into her black leather portfolio.

But it wasn't okay. Not one bit.

CHAPTER FOUR

Tori and Kallista were celebrating the fact that the school week was halfway through with a quick jaunt to the Galleria. Kallista had permission to come home with Tori after school to do homework, and they hardly had any.

They were laughing over the two T-shirts they had had made at the T-shirt kiosk in the middle of the mall. They were black with the words "FREE ALYSSA!" lettered in white. They had put them on in the bathroom at one of the designer stores — with the added bonus of a chance to drool over the cool shoes on their way back out to the mall.

Even cooler, they had totally scored at Suncoast Video, finding two of Cameron Stevenson's early films in the DVD remainder bin. Tori wanted to be up on every aspect of Michael's life, including his dad's movies.

With a plastic sack containing *Club Weirdo* and *I Know*

Who You Killed Last Summer slung over Tori's shoulder, the two friends were about to swing out the exit. But just as they reached the big double doors, Kallista grabbed Tori's arm.

"You are not going to believe who is coming up behind you," she whispered into Tori's ear. "Your leading man in *My Big Fat Sushi Wedding*."

"No way," Tori breathed.

"Way. Here he comes. In three, two, one...action!"

"Hey," Michael said, as Kallista oh-so-casually moved away from Tori to give her some space.

Tori's legs turned to Tofu Lite as she turned around. The blond hair. The blue eyes. He was wearing khaki cargo shorts and a dark blue T-shirt.

Ducking his head slightly, he put his hands in his pockets and came up to her, so closely that she could smell his shampoo.

"Hi," Tori managed. "Well. Fancy meeting you here." *Cringe – that is so lame!*

He smiled as if she had just said the wittiest thing he had ever heard. Butterflies started to party in her stomach.

He's just a guy, she reminded herself. *A person my age, who happens to be the adorable-est...cutest...Michael-est!*

He grinned and said, "I like your T-shirts. Alyssa's your friend in New Jersey, right?"

"Free Alyssa!" Kallista cried. "These shirts are going to be the next Hollywood trend. We're going to take a pic of ourselves at Tori's house and put it up on her camp blog."

"Sweet," he said, chuckling.

"We could get you one, too," Tori said, feeling a little shy. Maybe he wouldn't want one. Maybe that was something only for Camp Lakeview girls and their girlfriends.

"That'd be kind of cool," he said.

"We can go do it now," she replied, trying not to sound too eager even though she was, well, eager.

"Rock," he said. "I'm in."

"The kiosk is at the other end of the mall. And you have to wait for about twenty minutes while they make it," she added, just in case he didn't realize that getting a shirt would involve some quality time.

"It's all good," he assured her. "My dad's on a shoot and my mom's not home. So I'm on my own."

"Then you can come to Tori's house with us and get *your* pic on the blog, too," Kallista said.

He nodded. "Okay. Let's do it."

They started walking down the centre of the mall, Tori in the middle. She was walking with Michael Stevenson. And he was coming to her house!

She was floating again!

* * *

About an hour later, Tori, Michael and Kallista breezed into Tori's house, flinging school backpacks and shopping bags onto the black leather sofa. They sailed into the family's private screening room in their matching FREE ALYSSA T-shirts.

"You guys put the first movie in," Tori told Michael and Kallista. "I'll go get some snacks."

"You got it," Michael said, as he took his father's old movies out of the Suncoast Video bag. "Let's see, let's start with *Club Weirdo*. My father was nineteen in this movie. *I'm* practically nineteen." He blinked at the disbelieving looks of his two fellow middle-schoolers.

"Okay, I'm almost thirteen," he admitted.

"Ooh, an older man," Kallista cooed. "Tori and I have just turned twelve. Watch out for this guy, Tori. He's super-sophisticated."

Michael held up the DVD container for *Club Weirdo*, which featured a publicity still of his father in a very bad orange wig and green make-up. "Like father, like son," he said.

Giggling, Tori trotted out of the screening room and into the French-style black and white kitchen. Her father was seated in the breakfast nook, drinking a bottle of Perrier and reading a contract.

"Hi, honey," he said. He looked at her T-shirt and chuckled. "Alyssa's your artist friend?"

"Yes." She opened the pantry in search of microwavable popcorn. "We all got them. Michael, Kallista and me. We're protesting her censorship. Do we have any Cheetos? Michael is an orange-food freak. Or maybe Doritos?"

"Michael's here?" her father asked.

"Yeah. Kallista and I ran into him at the mall. His dad is night-shooting and his mom's got a thing. Can he stay for dinner?"

She snagged a bag of microwave popcorn and ripped the protective wrapper from it. As she carried it to the microwave, she smiled expectantly at her father.

But her father didn't smile back. In fact, he glanced down at the contract he had been reading, and then back up at her.

"Tori," he said slowly, "Michael's a nice kid. But..."

Tori opened the microwave door. "But what?"

"His father's a client of mine now. So it would be best if you two just saw each other around school."

Tori's cheeks burned. "All we did was go to the mall," she protested. "We're just going to watch movies and do homework."

He gave his head a shake. "Honey, you're not in trouble or anything. I just want you to keep some distance. You know how things are in this town. Success in the entertainment industry often depends just as much on who you know as much as how good you are at your job."

"Are you saying Michael's a user?" she asked, feeling even more defensive. "Because no offence, Daddy, but his father is a really famous movie star and he does *not* need to use me or you to make himself more famous!"

Her father pursed his lips, as if he wanted to say something more but was forcing himself not to. He took a slow drink of Perrier. "I'm not making myself clear," he said. "It's okay to be Michael's friend, but keep it light. Deal?"

He smiled at her as if he had made perfect sense. Which he had not.

"Okay," she mumbled.

"Besides, you're only in the seventh grade. That's a little young for anything besides a casual friendship."

She wanted to die of embarrassment. She could not believe she was talking to her father about a boy. While she microwaved the popcorn, she searched through the pantry for more snacks. Her stomach was in a knot, and she didn't even know why.

Yes, I do know why. I don't want to treat Michael as a Friend Lite. I'm crushing on him. I want him to be my first-ever serious boyfriend. Seventh grade is way old enough for that.

By the time she found a bag of Nacho Doritos and grabbed three sodas, she was actually near tears. But she forced them away and plastered on a big smile, dumping the popcorn, the Doritos and the sodas on a big tray and trotting back to the screening room as if she didn't have a care in the world.

To: Alyssa
From: Tori
Subject: FREE ALYSSA

Dear Lyss,
     Look at us! This jpeg is of my friends Kallista and Michael and me. We wore these T-shirts to school today to protest your teacher's unfairness! LOL! Some other kids said they're going to go to the mall over the weekend and get some made, too!
     FREE ALYSSA!
     Your friend,
     Tori

To: Tori
From: Alyssa
Subject: Re: FREE ALYSSA

Dear Tori,

That is so sweet! Thank you. Your T-shirt really cheered me up! Please thank your friends.

Yours in Art,

Lyss

It was Thursday, a rainy, cold day that matched Priya's mood. She kept her hands stuffed in her dark blue jacket as she and Jordan walked to school together, just like always. Her breath was leaving vapour trails and Jordan was babbling on about Brynn again.

"Jordan, we still don't have a topic," she said, feeling desperate. "Would you *please* just take a moment out of your total obsession with Brynn and work with me here?"

"It's not that hard. We'll do it on grossness!" he said, snapping his fingers. "Like, why is mucus gross but grape jelly isn't? They both have a high slime factor, so why do we eat grape jelly but we don't eat mucus?"

"Jordan, be serious!" she shouted.

"I am serious," he said. "We can get a whole bunch of disgusting stuff and—"

"We can not! We've been over this. No farts and no mucus. Don't you get how important this is?"

"Yeah, I do," he said, frowning at her. "What is up with you? We can investigate all the stuff we're really into! Boogers, scabs..." He wrinkled his nose. "It'll be awesome. It's all good, Priya."

"It's not all good," she said. "Jordan, that is a stupid topic and Ms. Romero will tell us it's wrong and – and I'm going to ask Ms. Romero to get me a different project partner!"

Whoa, where did that come from?

"*What?*" He stopped walking. "Priya, are you kidding me?"

"No." Her throat was dry, and she cleared it. She gave her head a little shake and said, "I can't risk getting a C for the semester. So..." She looked back up at him. "I think it would be better if we got other partners."

He blinked at her. "Priya, I'm Jordan. Your best friend. Are you actually dumping me?"

"You haven't been acting like a best friend!" she said. "Ever since we agreed to do this, you've been all, 'What can I get Brynn for her birthday?' 'What can I get Brynn for election day?' 'What can I get Brynn for the third Friday of the month?' 'Brynn, Brynn, Brynn,' and IMing her when you're supposed to be talking to me, and I am really tired of it!"

He looked at her like she was from another planet.

"You're serious," he said.

"I am. I totally am. I have been sitting around all week and—"

"Fine." He stomped off ahead of her. "No problem!"

"Right!" she yelled after him.

And I am right. This is the very best thing for me to do.

She walked the rest of the way alone. She went to her locker alone. She ate lunch alone.

Then she got to the science lab early. Ms. Romero was at her desk, grading quizzes from some other class. She looked up and smiled when she saw Priya.

"Hi, Priya," she said. "How's your project going?"

Priya balled her fists. Going? As in nowhere?

"Okay, the truth is, we haven't gotten very far," Priya confessed. "And...I was hoping you might assign me to someone that's better, I mean, stronger, in science."

"It's not working out?" Ms. Romero asked.

"No," Priya said. She raised her chin. "It really isn't."

Ms. Romero looked thoughtful as she nodded. "Okay. Let's try a new partner. Leslie's got a great project. I've already approved it. But it's very ambitious and she could use some help. Would you be interested in working with her?"

"Wow," Priya blurted. A chance to be on the same team as the queen of the science fair? "Yes, sure!" Then she thought a minute. "Does *she* want to work with *me*?"

"Well, she mentioned to me that she was sorry she

signed up to work alone. And I think you two would make a great team. Let's talk to her during class, all right?"

Priya licked her lips and glanced at the door. The students were beginning to trickle in.

"Okay," she said, "but can we do it so Jordan won't hear?"

"Of course," Ms. Romero said kindly.

To: Val
From: Priya
Subject: My New Partner

Hi, Val,

I changed science fair partners today and Jordan is really mad at me about it. I'm going to help this girl Leslie with her experiment on photosynthesis. It's a very cool project. We are going to use different kinds of light filters, like polarized lenses or UV-blocking sunglasses, to see if it affects how the plants grow. She is the smartest girl in our class and I am really lucky to be on her team.

When J found out, he told Ms. Romero he didn't want a new partner. He's going to do "our" experiment alone. He wouldn't even look at me in class and he didn't wait for me after school. Whatever! But what if Brynn gets mad at me too, because she's in loooove with him? This stinks.

— Priya

To: Priya
From: BrynnWins
Subject: NOT mad at you!

Dear Priya,

Val e-mailed me. I am NOT mad at you. I did IM Jordan about it and he said he didn't want to talk about it. I hope it all works out.

STILL YOUR FRIEND,

Brynn

On Friday in science, Jordan handed Ms. Romero a familiar thick packet and sat all the way across the room from Priya. He didn't look at her, didn't say a thing to her.

Fine, she thought, feeling defensive. Ms. Romero would take one look at his proposal and flunk him for the semester.

I got out just in the nick, she thought.

Leslie was sitting on Jordan's old stool. She looked up from writing down every single word Ms. Romero said and whispered, "I like your blouse."

"Thank you," Priya replied. It was a black and white Indian print, and one of Priya's favourites. Jordan said it looked like amoebas.

"We should get together and start working on the project after school," Leslie continued.

"I have to help my mom at the food court for a little while," Priya replied.

"Well, I live close to the mall," Leslie told her. "Maybe your mom could drive you over, and we could take you home."

"Great," Priya said. She added, "I like your blouse, too," even though it was just a plain red T-shirt and there was a little stain on the arm.

They walked out of the lab together. Jordan was still on his stool, gathering his books. She could tell he was stalling so he wouldn't have to walk out with her.

Fine.

Kids were gathering in the corridor, yakking about their weekend plans. She and Jordan usually did stuff like watch movies with her brother and shoot some hoops. She didn't suppose they'd be doing anything like that this weekend. Her throat felt a little funny as she imagined a weekend without Jordan.

Just then Marco Rubio fell into step beside Leslie. His backpack was so heavy it was pulling his shoulders down. He had more books in his arms.

"Graff," he said. "How's the project?"

"Good," she replied, with a little lift of her chin. Her cheeks were red. "Priya has joined my team."

He nodded at Priya. "Good thing you dumped Jordan. That guy is going nowhere in science."

"Hey, that's not true," Priya said. "And I didn't... dump him. He's still my friend."

"Oh, really?" Marco raised his brows. "I see." He inclined his head at Leslie. "Later, Graff."

"Bye," Leslie said softly.

Jordan is my friend, Priya thought.

Just then, Jordan stomped on past her without saying a word.

She gulped. *Okay, maybe he's not.*

CHAPTER FIVE

To: Alyssa
From: Juan Garcia-Paz
Subject: Ode to a Woman

Muy estimada Alyssa,

I am writing you to say that I love your picture,
Ode to a Woman. My friend Nani sent it to me. I
hope you do not mind that I write to you.

Best wishes from Spain!

— Juan G.P.

"That was good. Let's try another one," Priya's mother
said. They were in Smoothie Town in the food court,
and Priya was trying to learn how to mix the beverages
on her mother's vast menu. Mrs. Shah had been unable
to narrow down her selections, so she had decided to

put them all on her menu until she figured out which ones were the most popular with her customers.

"Razz-a-coco-rama," Priya read, trying to decipher the tiny font her mother had used to print out the directions. "Coconut milk, orange sherbet, raspberries." She crossed to the freezer and opened it. Inside were frozen bags of all the different kinds of fruit required for the drinks. She looked through them, finding blueberries, strawberries, mango purée and pineapple. "Um, I don't see the raspberries."

"Oh, darn it. I left them in the cooler in the car," her mother said, tapping her forehead. "I forgot to bring the last load in." Her mom had been organizing everything for her big opening night, and she was really stressed.

"I'll get it," Priya offered, holding her hand out for the keys.

"Thank you, sweetheart. You're a lifesaver," her mother said.

Priya put on her coat, took the big red twisty key chain from her mother's outstretched hand, and ducked under the counter.

Inside the food court, the other establishments were doing a brisk business. There were stalls for hot pretzels, fancy French fries, Chinese food, hot dogs with all kinds of toppings, pizza and pasta, and an ice cream place. The ice cream place was the only real competition her mom would have.

Priya jogged outside into the windy parking lot and unlocked the van. She found the green cooler on the floor and hefted it out. It wasn't very heavy. Then she set it on the ground so she could lock the van.

As she picked the cooler back up and headed back for the mall, she skidded on a patch of ice.

She squealed as she tried to find her footing. Then suddenly, a voice behind her said, "Hold on. I've got it."

A tall guy about her age walked up from behind her and took the cooler out of her grasp. He was seriously cute. His skin was the colour of hot chocolate and his eyes were brown with gold flecks in them. There were dimples on either side of his mouth and one in his chin.

"Thank you," she said.

"No problem." He cocked his head at her. "You're Smoothie Town. I'm Riley."

"Hi," she said, a little shy. "I'm Priya, actually."

He grinned at her. "My uncle owns Simpson's Hot Dogs. I help out now and then. So we're food-court neighbours."

"Oh." She liked that. She pulled the big glass door to the mall open for him and he drew back, allowing her to go in first.

They wiped their feet and then headed for the brightly lit, red-and-yellow-themed food court. Priya's mother looked up, then smiled when Riley set down the cooler and said, "I'm Riley Simpson. My uncle owns the hot dog place."

"How nice," she said, sounding distracted. Then she turned to Priya. "Honey, I just got a call from Sam. He's been injured at hockey practice. I have to go get him."

"Oh, no," Priya said. "Is it bad?"

"Well, they've got his leg iced and elevated and he could talk to me on the phone, but he sounds like he's in a lot of pain. I can drop you off at your friend's," she said, "but it may be a while until I can pick you up."

"Maybe she can come here," Priya suggested. "That way, if you're really late, I won't be in her family's way."

"I don't want to leave you here unsupervised," her mother said.

"Mom, it's just the mall," Priya protested.

"I have one kid down," Mrs. Shah said. "I'm not letting anything happen to my other one."

"Hang on a sec," Riley said. He bounded over to the hot dog place and spoke to an older man with a dark complexion and a thin moustache. He pointed to Priya and her mother.

The older man came over. "Hi, I've been meaning to welcome you to the food court," he said. "I'm Martin

Simpson. Riley and I would be happy to entertain your daughter while you check on your son. Riley can give you a hand with setting up your smoothie bar if things get slow at our hot dog counter," he added.

"Oh, that's very generous," her mother said, looking so relieved that Priya gave her a quick hug. Her mom was already so nervous, and now this.

"Hold on," Priya said. "Let me call Leslie."

She had written Leslie's address and phone number on a piece of paper. She quickly dialled while her mother started putting on her coat.

Leslie answered the phone right away.

"Hi! Are you on your way?" she asked Priya.

"Leslie, I'm so sorry, but can you come to the mall to work?" Priya asked her. She explained the situation, including the fact that her mom had to leave.

"Okay," Leslie answered after checking with her mom. "We can use one of the food court tables as a desk."

"Great. See you soon."

Priya disconnected and nodded at her mom. "Leslie's coming here," she told her.

But Mrs. Shah still looked a little worried.

"It'll be okay, Mom," Priya said.

"I'll...all right," her mother said finally. "Keep my cellphone and call home if you need *anything*, all right, honey?"

"I will," Priya promised.

Her mother left and suddenly she and Riley were by themselves. "Alone at last," Riley said, and Priya almost got the nervous giggles. But she kept herself pulled together as they both ducked under the counter and entered the land of Smoothie Town.

"What can I do?" he asked.

She just stared at him. And *smelled* him. He smelled really good, as if he had freshly showered, and his dark hair was really shiny.

He said, "What?" and pulled his chin in slightly, like he was trying to see what she was staring at. He lifted the tub of frozen raspberries out of the cooler.

"I was...just wondering what school you go to," she said. *Good save!*

"I go to Waggenheim."

"That's *my* school," she said.

"Huh. I've never seen you in any of my classes," he told her.

"Maybe you just never noticed me," she replied.

"No way." His tone was warm, and she went all mushy inside. "Are you an eighth-grader?"

She shook her head. "Seventh."

"Then that explains it. I'm an eighth-grader." He sounded very proud of that fact.

"Cool," she said.

"Not as cool as this." Before she knew what was happening, he reached around her and slipped a piece of ice from the cooler down her back!

"Evil!" she cried, grabbing at her back with both hands, trying to stop the sliver of ice from making a ski run down her backbone. When she gave up in defeat, she picked up a cup of water on the counter and flung it at him. Then she realized that it wasn't water – it was coconut milk!

"Oh, I'm so sorry!" she told him, as he blinked at her in surprise.

"No." He licked his chin. "This is interesting. What is it?"

"Coconut mi—" she began, just as he picked up the peel from a banana and tossed it at her. But this time she was too quick for him. Squealing, she caught it in mid-throw and tossed it back at him.

He plucked it out of the air as they both started shrieking, doubling over in laughter.

"Hey, you two, you might want to settle down a little," said a voice behind Priya. It was Riley's uncle. He was smiling at them, but Priya could tell he meant business.

"Sorry," Riley said. Then, after a beat, he added, "She started it."

"I did not!" She smacked Riley's arm. When he winced hard, she cried, "Oh, I'm sorry! Did I hit you too hard?"

He snorted. "Please."

"Kids, really, calm down, okay?" Mr. Simpson said. Then a lady with two little kids walked up to the hot dog stand and he left to take her order.

Riley stuck out his lower lip and said to Priya, "You got me in trouble."

"Oh, right." She giggled. She hadn't had a good laugh like this in a long time. Things had gotten pretty serious lately, what with the Jordan situation.

They found a bunch of stuff to unpack and organize in the little stock room in the back. Riley showed Priya some of the tricks of the trade, like putting a piece of coloured paper in your stacks of napkins and paper plates so you would notice when you were getting low. He also told her that they would have to be very, very careful about leaving food supplies out.

"Rats," he told her.

"No way." She made a face.

"Way."

They returned to the counter area. Priya searched the crowds for Leslie, but she hadn't shown yet.

Then her mom's cellphone went off. The caller ID was her dad's cellphone number.

"Hi, honey." It was her mom. "We're on our way to urgent care."

"What happened?" Priya asked. "How's Sam?"

"His coach thinks he broke his leg."

"Oh, no!"

"Yes. Poor Sam." Her mom took a breath. "I hate to ask this of you, Priya, but you know Smoothie Town is opening in a week. If Sam's going to be on crutches, I'm going to need some extra help."

"Mom, of course," Priya said. "I'll do whatever I can. I'll even skip school."

Her mother chuckled. "Nice try. And thank you, sweetie. I appreciate it. You won't have to skip school, but you might have to work over the weekend."

"No problem," Priya assured her. "Riley and I unpacked a bunch of stuff." She told her everything they had done.

"Thank you." Her mom sounded very appreciative, and that made Priya feel good.

"Oh," Priya said, as she spotted Leslie. She was standing in front of the food court sign in a heavy green jacket wearing her backpack. A woman who looked just like her – ponytail and glasses – stood beside her, holding a big cardboard box.

"Leslie just showed up," she told her mother.

"Okay. Get your work done. Call me later, all right?

84

Just to check in. Hopefully we'll have more information on Sam's leg."

"Tell him I hope he feels better," Priya said, worried about him.

As she disconnected, she said to Riley, "They think my brother broke his leg."

"Oh, *man*," Riley said, grimacing. "That's a bummer."

"Yeah. My mom's grand opening is next week, too."

"We'll help you," Riley promised.

Priya smiled. The she waved at Leslie, catching her eye, and Leslie waved back. She and the woman walked over.

Leslie said, "This is my mom."

"Hello. You must be Priya," Leslie's mom said.

"Yes, and this is Riley. His uncle owns the hot dog stall," she said.

"Are you on the science fair team?" Mrs. Graff asked him.

"No," Riley replied. "I'm more of an English and history person."

"Oh." Mrs. Graff shrugged as if Riley had just ceased to exist. She indicated the box in her arms and said to Leslie, "Well, honey, where shall I put this?"

"It's notes I've already taken," Leslie explained to Priya. "Just basic research. I put everything on file cards and then I input them once I can see my way through the information."

She looked around at the food court tables and pointed to one near the Indian food stall. She said, "How about there, Mom? I'll go get the rest."

"There's *more*?" Priya blurted.

"Oh, yeah. I found some phenomenal sources," Leslie said. Her eyes shone. "This is going to be the *best* science fair project I've ever done!"

"I've"? Not "we've"? Priya thought a little anxiously.

"Leslie's an old hand at science fairs," Mrs. Graff announced as she gazed at her daughter with pride. "Before we moved, she went to a science and technology magnet-school. Her room is just filled with science fair trophies." She gave Leslie's cheek a pat. "I'm sure she'll soon have another one to add to the collection."

"Oh, Mom," Leslie said, rolling her eyes. But it was pretty obvious she agreed.

"I'll carry that box over to the table for you," Riley offered.

"And I'll take your backpack," Priya said.

"Thanks. Here." Leslie slipped off the straps and handed the pack to Priya. Priya's knees buckled. It was amazingly heavy. "What's in here?"

"A few basic texts," Leslie said. She grinned at Priya. "I hope your school library card's got some space on it. I've checked out my limit, and there's a couple more we're going to need."

"Right. My card's good. We have room for lots of books." Possibly because she hadn't checked any out lately.

"Great." Leslie rubbed her hands together. "I'll go get the other box out of the car. Can you work maybe two hours? My mom can give you a ride home."

"Anything for the cause," Mrs. Graff said.

"I'm not sure. My brother broke his leg, so my parents are taking him to urgent care," Priya said.

Leslie tapped her chin. "Oh. They'll be there forever. What about three hours?"

Three hours? On a Friday night?

With the girl who is going to rescue me from getting a C in science? she reminded herself.

"I'm supposed to check back in a while to see how my brother is," Priya said. "I'll ask then."

"Okay, then." Leslie beamed at Priya. "I'll be right back."

Priya and Riley walked to the empty table Leslie had selected and Riley set down the box.

He said, "Wow, is all this for the Tri-County Regional Science Fair?"

She cocked her head. "I guess so. We're brand-new partners. I had a different partner but that didn't work..." She trailed off.

Heavily bundled against the cold, Jordan was walking past the food court. He was alone, and he looked like he was in a hurry. He didn't see her...or if he did, he pretended not to.

"I had a different project partner," she said, "but he was kind of a slacker."

Riley perched on the edge of the table and crossed his arms. He was so seriously cute.

"It's hard to work in groups," he said.

Just then Leslie bustled back in alone, carrying a box identical to the one on the table.

Gulp.

Riley straightened. "Well, I'd better let you two get to it." He slung his thumbs in his pockets and added, "Are you going to be here tomorrow?"

Ohmigosh! Priya couldn't believe it. A very cute, nice eighth-grader wanted to know if she was going to be there tomorrow!

"Maybe," she said.

"Cool," he replied. Then he walked back to his uncle's hot dog stand.

Priya watched him go. She wanted to hop up and down or squeal or something, but she kept herself under control. She wanted to ask someone if asking if she was going to be there tomorrow meant he was *interested* in her, or if it just meant he was nice.

"Leslie," she said excitedly, as the other girl reached the table.

"Amazing, isn't it?" Leslie said, setting the second box down beside the first. "And this is just the beginning. We are going to kill the competition! Especially Marco Rubio," she said, with a funny little smile. "He dares to tread on my subject matter! *I* thought of photosynthesis first."

"Right," Priya said. She grinned. "Listen, Leslie, Riley—"

"Okay. Let the games begin," Leslie said, opening the first cardboard box. "We're going to have to hustle if you only have three hours. Once I stayed up for two days straight on a project. It was worth it, though." She nodded at the memory.

Priya sensed this was not the time to discuss Riley.

"Okay," she said. "Let's hustle. Since we only have... three hours."

It was Friday afternoon. After Valerie settled herself in the corner of the dance room to do her homework during LaToya's class, she flipped open her folder and pulled out the print she had made of Alyssa's awesome painting-poem thingie. It was amazing to her that someone her own age – someone she *knew* – was so talented. And she was thrilled that her story about Ugandan women had inspired it.

"What's that?" LaToya asked, trying to peer over her shoulder.

Valerie put it back in her notebook. "Nothing."

LaToya sniffed. "Fine. I don't want to see it anyway."

Manzuma strode into the room with her dance skirt whirling around her long legs, and the advanced girls all lined up at the ballet barre. She looked so excited that she was actually glowing. "Girls, I have exciting news!" she said. "Ashanti Utu is going to be in town next week."

The advanced students all squealed and clapped their hands, jumping up and down.

"Who's that?" Valerie asked.

Seeing her expression, Manzuma explained, "Ashanti Utu is a world-famous choreographer and modern dancer. She's an old friend of mine. She lives in Paris and I haven't seen her in years."

"Will she be coming to the studio?" LaToya asked.

Manzuma nodded. "Not only that, but I want to mount a recital for her. It'll be on Saturday, a week from tomorrow, here at Fusion Space. I'll use the three animal dances the company dancers have been learning, plus I'll give four students the opportunity to present original works. That'll round our recital out nicely."

LaToya sucked in her breath. "We're going to perform our own work for her?" she cried, all total drama.

"*If* your piece is selected," Manzuma said, amused at LaToya's assumption that her dance would be one of those chosen.

LaToya didn't even register Manzuma's comment. Her eyes were shining. Valerie could practically see the visions of greatness dancing in her head.

"All right, ladies, enough," Manzuma said over the hubbub as the girls chattered among themselves. "We'll have a short warm-up and then I'll give you some time to start working on your dances. You only have a week to choreograph and learn them, so don't make them too complicated."

As the girls settled down, she walked over to her boom box. She hit Play and fantastic tribal music vibrated through the air.

"Please do your plié combination," Manzuma said, picking up her stick.

She began to pound out the rhythm of the music. As the class began to move, Valerie found her eyes drawn back to Alyssa's poem.

Hey, wait...

What if each word of Alyssa's poem was a dance step? And all the steps together could be the dance of her poem! Her poetry dance!

Valerie's entire body tingled. She knew she had a great idea. She could just *feel* how creative it was. *I can do this. It'll be just amazing!*

Watching LaToya's class go through their paces, she thought about what steps she would perform for each word. She decided to include some ballet moves. For "I" she would use the pose that had inspired Alyssa – the model standing with her hands up in the air, her back slightly bent. For "am" she would cross her hands over her chest.

Yes. I see the whole thing!

She spent the entire class mapping out her steps in her mind. She couldn't wait to actually try them out; to perform her dance for Manzuma in her class. Her heart was pounding with excitement.

I'm in the zone, just like Alyssa was, she thought. *I'm creating art!*

LaToya's class finally ended. As soon as the advanced girls cleared the dance space, Valerie leaped up and started stretching. She wanted to be warmed up and ready to go. She had a lot of dancing to do!

Manzuma left the room for the break between classes. LaToya stayed behind and primped in the mirror, checking her cornrows and reapplying her red lipgloss.

Gazing at Valerie in the mirror, LaToya said, "I can't believe you didn't know who Ashanti Utu is."

"So Ashanti Utu-sue me," Valerie replied, giggling. She was too happy to let LaToya bug her.

The beginning students trickled in and wandered over to the barre. Valerie eagerly joined them. Then Manzuma pushed through the beaded curtain, silently counting the number of girls as she walked over to the boom box.

As her hand hovered over the Play button, she said, "Girls, I have a wonderful announcement. Ashanti Utu will be visiting our studio. The advanced class will put on a recital for her a week from Saturday. You and your families are welcome to attend. I'll make up a flyer you can take home."

Then she punched on the music.

"Let's start with some stretches," she told the class. "Does everyone remember how to do a plié?"

Valerie's lips parted in dismay. The beginners' class wasn't being given the chance to create dances for the recital! She quickly raised her hand.

"Aren't we going to try out for the recital?" she asked.

"No, dear," Manzuma said. "Just the advanced class."

Not fair!

LaToya smirked at her. "Soften your fingers," she said under her breath as she ambled past Valerie. "They look like claws."

CHAPTER SIX

Posted by: Val
Subject: Excited & frustrated!

You know how I'm taking dance at LT's studio? Well, the teacher announced that this famous dancer is coming to the studio in two weeks and she's picking four dances for the students to show her.

So I came up with the coolest thing – I took Lyss's poem and I made a step up for each word. It is totally awesome! But then I found out that the beginners' class isn't allowed to try out!

Now all LT talks about is how she's gonna blow the competition out of the water and get discovered and move to France. I am trying to ignore her, but she is loving telling everyone at school that I'm in the baby class and all we get to do is watch "the real dancers".

What do you think I should do?

Trying to stay chilly,

Val

To: Val
From: Jenna
Subject: Re: Excited & frustrated!

Hi, Val,

I'm so glad you like dance again! Awesome! Maybe you could put on some music and do your dance before your class, and then your teacher would see it. What do you think?

Your friend,

Jenna

PS: I think you are doing an awesome job of dealing with LT.

To: Val
From: NatalieNYC
Subject: follow your dream!

val, it is so cool that you created a dance from lyss's poem! why don't you show it to manzuma

96

anyway? my dad always says that the reason he became a famous actor was that he never gave up. he asked to audition for the first spy movie and everyone kept saying no. but he kept asking and finally the director said okay just to shut my dad up! and my dad got the part! and the rest is history.

do the same thing! then you might be on dancing with the stars with my dad! lol!

love,

nat

To: Val

From: BrynnWins

Subject: Re: follow your dream!

Val, I suggest you show Manzuma your dance! The worst that can happen is that she will tell you that she doesn't like it.

Just Do It!

Your friend,

Brynn

To: Val

From: Candace

Subject: take a chance

I say, go for it!
TTFN,
Candace

Posted by: Alyssa
Subject: FREE ALYSSA!

Hello, everybody,

The most amazing thing has happened. I have started getting e-mails from kids all over the world about my *Works* contest entry! Some of them have sent me pictures of themselves in black T-shirts with white letters, like Tori and her friends. Do you guys know how this happened?!

I'm not sure what to do, but it's been really nice to read so many letters of encouragement. I'm trying to answer all of them, but there are a lot!

Yours in Art,
Lyss

Posted by: NatalieNYC
Subject: FREE ALYSSA!

hi, lyss and everyone,

guilty of spreading the word! i told some of

my friends at school, and hannah e-mailed a few people. hannah's mom is an ambassador and she has e-mail friends all over the world. so then those friends e-mailed their friends and it looks like it's become a chain! somehow your e-mail addy must have gotten added. (hope it's okay!)

this is just more proof of how awesome your pic is!

love,

nat

Alyssa worked all weekend to come up with another entry for the *Works* contest. She ransacked her closet, where she had kept *every* sketch she had *ever* done, and looked through them for hours. Some of them were pretty good, but nothing matched *Ode to a Woman*.

She even tried to jazz up *Flowers at Dawn*. After her talk with Mr. Prescott, she understood what was wrong with it. He was right. She had tried to play it safe by creating something no one could possibly object to. So instead of expressing herself, of showing the world a part of Alyssa, she had...painted some pretty flowers.

So she gave up on it.

By Sunday night, she had come up with no new

contest submission. She quickly did the rest of her homework, and then she logged on to check her e-mail one last time.

To: Alyssa
From: Marianne LaTour
Subject: Ode to a Woman!

Beautiful Alyssa,
   I see the picture, I hear your story of courage. I salute you! I am French girl, I think you are so brave! Keep the fight! And such good the artiste!
   T'A! (In France, we say "t'amie", your friend!)
   Marianne

Alyssa opened the attachment of a girl around her own age holding a print of *Ode to a Woman* and a banner that said FREE ALYSSA!

Now I've had e-mails from several different states and a couple of continents. I'm internationally famous, Alyssa thought, writing a quick thank you and shutting down. *But I'm still no closer to being published in* Works.

It was Sunday night, and Priya was exhausted. The weekend was a blur. The only time she had not worked on the science fair project was when she 1) did homework for her other classes; 2) helped her mom at Smoothie Town (which was cool, because that was when she got to talk to Riley); or 3) waited on Sam and tried to cheer him up.

She didn't think she had actually slept.

But it's all good, she thought, yawning as she sat at her PC and checked her e-mail one last time. *Because I have a science fair project and I'm in total crush mode!*

She wanted so badly to tell someone. She just wasn't sure who. In the old days, pre-science fair, Jordan would have been the first to know. But Jordan and she weren't speaking.

It felt horrible and weird, especially when Priya found out that he had come over to see Sam on Saturday when she was at the mall.

"Did Jordan even mention my name?" she asked Sam as she handed him the remote control. He had a habit of kicking it off the side of his bed.

"Um...not really, we mostly just talked about athlete's foot and earwax," Sam answered, snickering.

Priya wondered if Ms. Romero had actually approved his lame-o topic for the science fair.

Then an e-mail arrived in her inbox.

Maybe it's from Jordan, she thought. *Apologizing to me.*

To: Priya
From: LGraff
Subject: Lunch tomorrow

Hi, Priya,

I think we had a good start on our project this weekend, but we've got a lot more to do. So let's get together at lunch tomorrow and get back to work, okay? If you bring a lunch instead of buying, we can save time.

— Leslie

Priya moaned. She thought about typing back, *Give me a break! Please!* But she held back. Leslie was kind of her last chance.

To: LGraff
From: Priya
Subject: Re: Lunch tomorrow

Dear Leslie,
I'll be there.
— Priya
PS: I'm sorry, but I didn't understand that section on polarized light that you asked me to read. :(Maybe we can talk about it at lunch?

Another message came in. Leslie must've been online.

To: Priya
From: LGraff
Subject: Polarization

Dear Priya,
What didn't you get? It's pretty straightforward stuff. Maybe take another look before bed? I'd like to move on with other stuff at lunch if poss.
— Leslie

"Oh, argh!" Priya cried as she finished reading the message. "Give me a *serious* break!"

She powered down her computer and climbed into bed. Then she remembered that Riley would be at school tomorrow, and she smiled a little. What would it be like at school between them? He was into being an eighth grader — would he treat her differently at school? Act one way at the food court, but when they were around their friends and classmates, act another way?

She thought about getting up and posting about it on her Camp Lakeview blog, but then she realized that Brynn would read it and she would probably tell Jordan.

Priya kind of wanted him to know, but also kind of didn't.

She sighed and rolled over, determined to get some sleep. After all, she was going to have a very busy day tomorrow.

In the morning, Alyssa got ready for school, bundling up for a blustery November day. Beckah and Rose knocked on the door, and Alyssa stepped out onto the porch. The sky was grey and it looked as if it might snow.

"Hi, guys," she said.

Beckah and Rose grinned at each other, and then each put a hand on one hip and moved her right shoulder forward, posing like a fashion model. Wrapped around the right sleeves of their heavy winter coats were black bands with FREE ALYSSA! written in white letters.

Alyssa giggled. "You know we're not supposed to wear slogans and stuff to school. You'd better take them off before we get there."

"No way! We're protesting," Beckah said. "My mom told me that when she was young, people held all kinds of political protests at their schools."

"Like in the civil rights movement," Rose added.

"Well, this is just about an entry for a contest," Alyssa reminded them.

"Not *just*," Beckah countered. "You have rights, too!"

Alyssa didn't know what to say to that. It *was* kind of thrilling to realize that people were standing up for her. It made her feel that they were taking her work seriously.

As they turned right and headed down the last block, the three-storey brick building that was West Hills Middle School came into view. In front of the school, about thirty students were standing in a clump, chanting something in unison. Some of them were carrying signs that said FREE ALYSSA NOW!

"Beckah! Rose! What's going on?" Alyssa cried.

"Listen to what they're saying," Beckah said.

"Free Alyssa now! Free Alyssa now!" the students were yelling.

Alyssa swallowed hard. "I can't believe how this all caught on," she said.

"You're like the censorship poster child," Beckah responded.

The yelling turned to cheers as the three friends stepped onto the crossing. Then someone pointed at Alyssa and shouted, "There she is!"

The chanting got louder: *"Free Alyssa now!"*

Then Alyssa said to Beckah and Rose, "Uh-oh. There *he* is."

Mr. Prescott was standing at the top of the stairs that led to the school with his arms folded across his chest. There was a satchel slung over his shoulder in place of his usual tower o' stuff. He was scowling at Alyssa.

The double doors to the school opened and Ms. Caya, the school principal, appeared beside Mr. Prescott. She was scowling at Alyssa, too. As Alyssa, Beckah and Rose drew near the bottom of the stairs, Rose clasped her mittened hand over her sleeve to hide her armband. But Beckah defiantly let hers show.

Once the protesting students realized that the principal had arrived, the cheers died down and eventually stopped. Everybody looked at one another nervously.

Ms. Caya said in a loud voice, "It's time for first period to begin. I will see *no* more signs, and anyone wearing slogans of any kind will be suspended for the rest of the week."

While Ms. Caya descended the stairs, Beckah and Rose quickly unpinned their armbands and slipped them into their pockets. Mr. Prescott came down one step behind Ms. Caya, and there was a wave of freak-out throughout the assembled students.

Ms. Caya's face was pinched with anger as she stopped in front of Alyssa. Mr. Prescott stood shoulder-to-shoulder with her, looking just as angry.

"Alyssa, in my office, please, *now*," Ms. Caya said. Both she and Mr. Prescott turned and started back up the stairs, obviously expecting Alyssa to follow.

Taking a deep breath, Alyssa looked one last time at her friends. Rose crossed her fingers and Beckah gave her a thumbs-up. She tried to smile her thanks but she was too nervous.

She went up the stairs, into the school, and down the hall towards the principal's office. Some of the other students glanced at her with raised eyebrows, as if they were trying to figure out what she was in trouble for. A boy with brown hair gave her a little wave and said, "Free Alyssa!"

Neither Ms. Caya nor Mr. Prescott appeared to have heard him, and she was relieved. Now was not the time, and her middle school was definitely not the place!

Alyssa hadn't been in the principal's office since, well, ever. It was smaller than she would have expected. The walls were covered with photographs of students, including a pretty girl in a maroon graduation cap and gown who looked like Ms. Caya. Alyssa wondered if she was Ms. Caya's daughter.

Ms. Caya swept behind her broad oak desk and sat

down in her chair. Mr. Prescott stood to one side, in front of a bookcase. The books had titles like *Challenges of Managing Youth* and *Redirecting Delinquent Behaviour.*

Gulp!

"Have a seat, please," Ms. Caya said to Alyssa.

Alyssa took off her backpack and set it on the floor. Then she sat down, folded her hands in her lap, and wondered what was going to happen next.

"Alyssa," the principal began, "Mr. Prescott explained to me that you tried to submit an inappropriate piece of art for the arts quarterly."

Yikes! That sounded so harsh!

Alyssa swallowed hard. "I didn't know it was inappropriate," she blurted. Then she took a deep breath and added, "I still don't understand what's wrong with it, to be honest."

"Be that as it may," Ms. Caya said, "what did you hope to accomplish by organizing a disruptive protest? Did you think it would make a difference?"

"I didn't organize it! Honest!" Alyssa replied. "I didn't know it was happening. I didn't ask anyone to do anything!"

"How do you explain this?" Mr. Prescott asked. He reached into his satchel and pulled out a black FREE ALYSSA T-shirt. "This was on my desk. And there was scribbling about free speech all over the whiteboard in the art room."

"I just got to school," Alyssa said. "I didn't put that on your desk, Mr. Prescott. I have a friend in California who made a T-shirt like that at a mall, and she sent me a jpeg. And I sent it to a few of *my* friends and..."

She trailed off, listening to how that sounded. She felt guilty, even though she hadn't actually done anything.

"I didn't know people were making more T-shirts, or signs, or anything." She had trouble looking at Mr. Prescott as she added, "And I didn't write anything on the whiteboard."

"We *did* just see her arriving at school," Mr. Prescott said, folding the T-shirt and putting it back in his satchel. "I'm willing to give her the benefit of the doubt."

Maybe that should have made Alyssa feel better, but it didn't. Because it sounded to her like Mr. Prescott still wasn't entirely convinced that she was innocent.

"All right," Ms. Caya said. "But I want you to explain to your friends that they may not do any more protesting. No T-shirts, armbands, or signs will be tolerated. No graffiti. Am I clear?"

"Yes. Very," Alyssa assured her.

The first bell rang. Mr. Prescott glanced at his watch and said, "I have a class."

"Me too," Alyssa added hopefully, wanting like anything to get out of the principal's office and back to her normal life. She couldn't imagine what it would feel like to be in trouble for real. Awful!

"Please go on ahead, Mr. Prescott," Ms. Caya continued. "Alyssa, I'd like you to stay a moment. I'll write you a hall pass."

Alyssa's stomach twisted as she remained seated. Mr. Prescott brushed past her chair, and she cringed, wondering how on earth she was going to handle being in art today. She was so upset. After Mr. Prescott had left, Alyssa looked anxiously at the principal. "I didn't know this was going to happen," she said again.

"I believe you," Ms. Caya replied, and Alyssa slumped with relief. "However," the principal continued, "what happens next is up to you. It's too bad that Mr. Prescott felt your artwork wasn't suitable for the contest, but—"

In her eagerness to ask her question, Alyssa interrupted, saying, "Have you seen it? Do *you* think it's unsuitable?"

Ms. Caya gazed steadily at her. "What I think doesn't matter," she said. "Mr. Prescott is the *Works* advisor."

"But...you're the *principal*," Alyssa ventured.

"Yes. I am. And I support Mr. Prescott's right to make this decision. Do I make myself clear?"

"Yes," Alyssa said.

"Why don't you try submitting a different piece?" Ms. Caya asked.

"I already have," Alyssa murmured. "I don't have anything as good."

"Well, you have until Friday to come up with something else." The principal smiled gently and reached for a pad of pink forms. "You're a talented girl, Alyssa."

"Th-thanks," Alyssa said, startled and pleased by the praise.

"Here's your hall pass," Ms. Caya said, checking off a couple of boxes and scribbling her signature at the bottom. She ripped the piece of paper off the pad and handed it to Alyssa. "Go on to class."

"Thank you," Alyssa said. She held on to the pass with one hand while she hoisted up her backpack with the other. Then she turned and left the room, entering the hall, where a few stragglers were still running to get to their classes.

She started walking. And then it dawned on her to wonder *how* Principal Caya knew she was a good artist. Had Mr. Prescott shown her some of her other work? Had she seen *Ode to a Woman*?

Probably not. Mr. Prescott had rejected it when Alyssa had shown it to him, and Alyssa had taken it directly home.

Maybe Ms. Caya had just said those nice things to cheer Alyssa up.

Well, it had worked. A little. Alyssa was still freaked out, but it was nice to hear an adult praise her artistic ability. She just wished she would have the chance to share *Ode* with the rest of the school.

And she wished she wasn't dreading seeing Mr. Prescott again. Whatever the case, she sure wasn't going to submit anything to an art contest ever again in her entire life!

CHAPTER SEVEN

It was lunchtime on Monday, and Tori and Kallista were eating falafel from Trader Joe's. Well, Kallista was eating it and Tori was rolling one of the little falafel balls back and forth in her tahini sauce, then making designs with it on her black plastic plate.

Michael had IM'd Tori three times over the weekend. And each time, she had pretended that she wasn't online. She had sat at her computer trying to figure out if it was okay if she talked with him. After all, she talked to lots of people online.

But she knew her dad wouldn't like it. So she hadn't replied. And she was bummed.

"Here comes Michael," Kallista told her.

"Is he smiling or frowning?" Tori asked her.

Kallista shielded her eyes with her hand. "I can't tell. The sun is blocking my view."

"Kallista, please! Don't be so obvious," Tori begged her under her breath.

"Hi," Michael said as he approached. He looked down at their lunch. "Yum. Falafel. I should have eaten with you guys instead of in the café." He smiled broadly at Tori, who dropped her gaze to her plate. She hoped he wouldn't notice that most of the designs she had made looked suspiciously like MS, Michael's initials.

"Um, yeah," Kallista said. "The café is a total bummer. That's why we always bring our lunch."

"You do? What are you having tomorrow?" Michael asked, slinging his thumbs into his jeans pockets. He looked directly at Tori.

Tori glanced at Kallista for help. She had no idea what to say. Kallista stared back at her, looking stuck, so Tori blurted, "Actually, I'm not having lunch tomorrow. I-I'm fasting. We fast once a month." She looked at Kallista.

"Right." Kallista shifted awkwardly. "Juice fast."

"Oh." He nodded. "But you still come out here for lunch."

"Yeah, but now we have to go to our lockers," Tori said. "Because we forgot our maths books."

Michael cocked his head. He had a kind of strained half-smile on his face. "Both of you?"

Tori nodded. "We do everything together. Share lunch, forget our books..."

Then she made herself stand up, sling her bag over her shoulder, and pick up her tray.

"See you later," she said.

"Okay." He brightened. "You busy after school?"

"Tennis lesson," Tori said. But she wanted to say, *I am not busy when it comes to you, Michael.*

"No, today's Monday, Tor. We have tennis tomor... oh, yeah, that darn new schedule," Kallista said quickly, as Tori threw her a look. She laughed the fakest laugh Tori had ever heard. It was a good thing Kallista had no interest in becoming an actress.

"Okay," Michael said slowly. He didn't follow after them as the two girls walked away.

"He's looking at you," Kallista informed Tori. "He looks upset."

"He looks how I feel," Tori murmured. What *was* she going to do?

"Hi, Priya," Riley said Monday at lunchtime as she shut her locker.

Whoa. He is at my locker. At lunchtime! That means serious like!

Doesn't it?

115

He looked really good in a black sweater and black jeans. Priya was amazed that she hadn't noticed the little stud in his left ear. She had stared at, er, seen him for several hours on Saturday and Sunday, when she had helped her mom.

And now...she knew he had an earring. *That is so cool!*

"Um, do you buy your lunch?" he asked her. "I'm buying today."

She winced inwardly. *This cannot be happening to me.* "I brought it. And I, um, have to work on the science fair project with Leslie. We're going over a few things."

He frowned a little, looking confused. "But I thought you worked on it over the weekend."

"Yeah, well." She moved her shoulders. "I have to catch up. She started this project weeks ago." *Make that months.*

"Oh. Oh, well." He just stood there beside her locker. She realized he was waiting for her. *Wow!* She was so excited!

"How's your brother?" he asked. "Did he break his leg?"

"Yes," she replied happily. Then she heard herself and added, "He has a cast on and he won't be able to help my mom out much. We were going to divvy up working at Smoothie Town, but now I'm the main worker bee."

"You're the double main worker bee," he said. "Making smoothies and working on science experiments."

"Yeah," she said. "I thought of that."

"So you'll be pretty busy," he continued.

She caught her breath. Was he going to ask her out? Like on a date?

"*There* you are," Leslie said, marching up to Priya. She was smiling but her voice was kind of...tense. "I've got us a table."

"O-kay," Priya said slowly. She looked at Riley.

Go ahead. Please. Ask me out!

"Catch you later," he said.

Argh.

"Polarization," Leslie said. "The light reflects against the prism and...Priya?"

Across the warm, steamy cafeteria, Riley was standing in line to pay for his lunch. Priya couldn't tell what was on the tray, except that he was buying *three* milks. Impressive!

"Priya?" Leslie said again.

"Sorry." Priya turned her attention back to Leslie. "Reflection."

"Yes." Leslie's hand roamed over some of the folders

she had fanned across their lunch table. There wasn't much room for actual food.

"Let's see...ah, here it is. Basic facts." She whipped open the folder marked PRINCIPLES and pulled out a big, thick, juicy handout. "Try this instead of the other article I gave you."

"Okay," Priya said. Now Riley was walking across the cafeteria towards a table of guys and girls. Lots of girls. Cute girls. One of them had red hair and big brown eyes; she smiled up at him and scooted out the empty chair next to her.

"No," Priya whimpered.

"Graff. Shah," said a voice behind her. It was Marco. He *tsk-tsk*ed. "All this work for second place. What a pity."

"You wish," Leslie said.

He came around Priya. He had bought lunch, too. It was mac and cheese. Priya loved the café's mac and cheese. Her mom hadn't gone to the store in a while, so Priya had made herself a PB&J on stale bread and unearthed an almost-bad apple from the crisper in the fridge. The apple reminded her of Jordan's rotten apple in his locker, and she felt sad.

Marco glanced down at the article Leslie was about to hand to Priya.

"Polarization? The effects of, as regarding photosynthesis? You're going for the *tired* and true, I see."

"Ms. Romero thinks it's very solid," Leslie retorted.

"I scoff," he said. Then he glided away.

The girl seated next to Riley threw back her head and laughed as if he had just said the funniest thing in the world.

That should be me, Priya thought.

Just then, she spotted Jordan coming through the metal double doors that led to the cafeteria kitchen. He was carrying a small metal dish, and he was wearing a big white apron and a hairnet!

Priya cracked up. She leaned over to Leslie and said, "Look at Jordan!"

"Priya! You need to focus!" Leslie snapped at her.

"Okay, sorry," Priya said. She settled in to read about polarization.

Why is he wearing an apron and a hairnet? she wondered. *And what's in the dish?*

"Reading," she said, grimacing. "Promise."

"So, are you ready to move on?" Leslie asked, tapping her fingers on the table.

"What?" Priya blinked and looked at the clock. Lunch was almost over. She hadn't even finished the first page of the article.

Because I haven't really been reading it, she admitted to

119

herself. It was boring, and she had a lot of distractions to deal with – her ex-best friend and the guy she hoped would be her future boyfriend.

The bell rang. Leslie muttered, "Well, *this* was a huge waste of time," and started cramming all her files back into another cardboard box. Priya tried to help, but Leslie gritted, "I have a system."

Then it was time for science lab. More science. Priya's eyes were crossed. The very thought made her want to run screaming in the opposite direction.

When she and Leslie entered the room, she saw Jordan standing in front of Ms. Romero's desk with the dish he had had in the cafeteria. Ms. Romero was holding her nose and *laughing*.

Jordan was laughing, too. Until he saw Priya. Then his smile faded. He slid the dish into a large plastic Ziploc bag and carried it to his new lab stool in the land of As Far Away From Priya As I Can Get.

"Hi, girls," Ms. Romero said to Priya and Leslie, who was struggling under the weight of her enormous cardboard box. "How's it going?"

"Oh, just *great*," Leslie said sarcastically. Then she slammed the box onto the floor beside her stool and climbed up on it.

Ms. Romero raised a brow but said nothing. Priya sat down on her stool, feeling like a total loser.

Then she felt someone staring at her. Someone like Jordan.

She took a breath and glanced over her shoulder.

But he was playing with the Ziploc bag, opening and closing it and talking to himself – or the dish, it was hard to tell – like a lunatic.

Her eyes welled. She missed that lunatic.

It was Monday after school, and it was time for Valerie to face the music – or rather, to dance to it.

LaToya went into the Fusion Works dressing room first, as if she was expecting Valerie to meekly follow behind so she could change into her koala-bear leotard. But Valerie sailed on past and into the dance room.

As she went, she peeled off her heavy dark blue sweater, revealing a stretchy blue velour top she had almost forgotten she owned. But she had found it when her father had asked her to take everything out of her wardrobe so he could pull up her ruined floor.

She had also worn some black bootcut trousers that looked almost like the jazz trousers she had seen on another dancer. Now she figured she actually *looked* like a dancer, instead of someone dressed in make-do clothes so she could take a few classes.

Manzuma was in the dance room, dancing alone to

some flute music. The director was very graceful, and Valerie paused to watch. She got even more nervous.

Manzuma noticed her, held her pose and said, "Hello, Valerie. Do you want something?"

Valerie hesitated. Then she said, "Yes. I do. I want a chance to show you my dance. I made one up to show Ashanti Utu."

"Oh?" Manzuma made a little face and dropped her hands to her sides as the music ended. "Your class isn't quite ready for performing, dear."

Valerie started to wilt. Then she remembered all the e-mails she had received from her friends. They believed in her. She had to believe in herself.

"Can I just show it to you?" Valerie asked. "I think you'll really like it, and like I said, I do have a lot of ballet experience." Manzuma didn't say anything. She just knit her brows and appeared to be thinking. Which was as good an indication as any to Valerie that she should continue her plea.

"What I did was, I took this poem a friend of mine wrote, and I gave each word a movement. So I dance the poem."

"Hmm. That's intriguing," Manzuma said. "True poetry in motion."

"Yes," Valerie said, flushing. "At least, I hope so."

Manzuma thought a moment. Then she nodded. "All

right, dear. Did you bring your music with you?"

"No. I don't have any," Valerie admitted. She had already thought through this problem. "But I think it would go very nicely with that plié music you use for the advanced class."

"Then I'll put it on," Manzuma said. "Go take your opening position."

Valerie was trembling as she walked to the centre of the dance floor. Manzuma clicked open the boom box and took out the CD that was already in it. Then she looked through a stack of CDs and put the correct one in.

The heavy bass rhythm vibrated through the floor and into the bones of Valerie's feet. It was as if the music were tapping her, saying, *let's go!*

Valerie performed her step for *I* – head and shoulders thrown back, arms reaching for the ceiling. Then *am*. She whirled in a circle.

Out of the corner of her eye, she caught the movement as the beaded curtain parted. Two of the advanced girls walked halfway through the curtain, then stopped. They were watching her intently.

No, she protested. *I don't want to dance in front of anyone but Manzuma!*

But she couldn't stop now. Valerie knew she had to stay focused. She crouched down, then leaped straight into the air. She whirled around again...and saw that *LaToya* had joined the other two girls.

No! Not LaToya! Valerie flared with anxiety and almost froze up. Her dance began to leave her head. Then she remembered that she was dancing for Manzuma, not LaToya, and pulled herself back together.

She kept dancing, performing each word in the poem, then repeated the entire poem to use up the music. *Yes*, she thought. *I like this!*

She finished the repeat, then held her pose for the rest of the music, which lasted about ten more seconds. Her chest was heaving. Sweat poured down her forehead. Her legs were shaking.

The music faded, and stopped.

Then there was loud applause and a couple of "Woo hoos!" Valerie looked across the room to see about half of the advanced class gathered at the perimeter of the dance floor, clapping and cheering.

LaToya, however, stood with her arms crossed, scowling.

Manzuma came up to Valerie, flung open her arms, and gave Valerie a big hug.

"Dear child!" she cried. "That was wonderful, Valerie. Highly skilled. Why didn't you dance like that at your audition?"

"Thank you," Valerie managed to say. She was stunned.

"I think you'd do better in the advanced class after all," Manzuma continued. "As of now, I'm reassigning you. And keep working on the piece, so that you're in tip-top shape for the audition on Friday."

"You think I have a chance?" Valerie blurted, practically swaying with joy.

"I do," Manzuma said with a chuckle. "So keep Saturday clear just in case."

She turned to the other girls and clapped her hands. "Time for class, girls! Valerie will be joining us." She walked across the room to retrieve her dance stick.

The other dancers drifted past Valerie to get to the barre. One patted her shoulder; one gave her a high five and said, "Way to dance, girlfriend!"

Another said, "Maybe I could dance your dance with you. We could do a duet."

LaToya walked towards the barre, her face flushing as one of the other girls said to her, "Your sister sure can dance!"

"*Step*sister," LaToya replied.

Then LaToya got into position in front of Valerie. She turned around and said in a low, angry voice, "Don't get too excited."

* * *

"It's time to go, Tori!" Tori's mother called to her. They were off to a combination sneak-premiere of Kallista's father's new sci-fi TV movie. The cable channel that was going to show the movie was filming the private premiere of the movie ahead of the broadcast on TV. They were going to use the footage for commercials and for when they showed the movie on TV.

They had asked everyone to dress up, and Tori and Kallista were more than happy to oblige. They had even planned coordinating outfits. Tori was wearing a dark pink frilly beaded dress with an asymmetrical hem and silver earrings and charm bracelet. Kallista was wearing a silver dress with all-pink jewellery.

"Tori?" her mother called again.

"Coming," Tori said as she hastily double-clicked on an e-mail from Natalie. She held her breath, hoping that Natalie could give her some much-needed words of wisdom. She was so confused. Michael had IM'd her a couple of times, and she hadn't responded. Then he left her a very sweet e-mail about not being able to connect. He finished it by saying, "Have I done something wrong?" So Tori had e-mailed Natalie, a fellow movie kid, to see if she could give her some guidance on how to 1) deal with a guy and 2) deal with a guy whose dad was in the film industry.

"Tori?" Now her *father* was calling her.

The message from Natalie popped open.

To: Tori
From: NatalieNYC
Subject: guys & hollywood

dear tori,

i completely understand what you are going through with michael. last year I couldn't figure out if kyle at school was asking me out on a date to go rollerblading or if it was just a friend thing. It turned out he wanted it to be a date. it sounds to me like that's what michael (and you!) want, too.

i also understand why your dad is being so super-cautious. one summer when i was in h-wood with my dad, this girl was really nice to me. it turned out her mom wanted a part in my dad's movie. when it didn't happen, she said she hated me and she only pretended to be my friend because of my dad. then her mom gave an interview to a magazine and told them private stuff about my dad that i had told her.

i am not saying that michael would ever do anything like that. i know michael is cool and his dad is famous, but my dad likes me to stick to my nyc buds cuz of what happened to me. i know it's harder for you to have non-industry buds cuz you live in cali 24/7!

i know this isn't much help, but at least you know i understand.

love,

nat

Tori sighed. Natalie was right. It wasn't much help. Well, except for the rollerblading date-that-really-was-a-date. That was good information. Natalie was right: she didn't think Michael wanted to be "just friends".

But maybe he does. You don't know yet.

And she wasn't sure how she would ever find out.

"Honey?" Tori's mother said from the doorway. She had on a beautiful calf-length red satin dress and dangling black earrings. "Important e-mail?"

Tori swallowed and nodded, hoping her mom wouldn't come over to her chair and look over her shoulder at her computer screen. She said, "Mom, do you think it's okay for people in the movie industry to date each other?"

She looked puzzled. "Well, yes. If they want to."

Tori smiled to herself. *Mom says yes!*

Then Tori's dad came up behind her, handsome in a black suit and white shirt. "What's holding up the show?" he asked.

"Nothing. I'm ready," Tori said, speaking first so her mom wouldn't have a chance to spill the beans about her question.

The limo whisked Tori and her parents off to the Arclight, a neat theatre often used for premieres. Sci-fi fans had been alerted to the event, and they were crammed behind barricades, searching for their favourite actors and actresses.

Tori was used to the way passers-by craned their necks to see if someone famous was inside the limo, then looked disappointed when it was Tori and her family. Fans didn't care about entertainment lawyers and their kids, but that was fine with Tori.

They walked down the red carpet that led into the theatre. Once inside the spacious lobby, Tori spotted Kallista with her parents. As they had planned, Kallista's gown was silver and her jewellery was silver with pink, glittery gems.

Kallista bounded over to her, giving her a hug. Their families joined up and went to their reserved seats inside the auditorium. The cast and crew were there, and when they saw Kallista's dad, they all cheered and whooped. Tori could not deny that it was awfully cool to be an industry kid, despite the problems that went with it.

The movie was also very cool — a swashbuckling space opera with lots of intricate computer-graphic spaceships and wicked-ugly aliens. Tori and Kallista shared a big tub of popcorn and a massive Diet Coke, and about halfway through the film, Tori had to go to the bathroom. So she excused herself, tiptoed out of the auditorium, and used the facilities.

She was just about to head back in when she heard someone softly calling her name.

"Tori?" It was Michael!

Tingles and chills washed over her as she turned around to face him. He was wearing black leather trousers and a white tailored shirt with the sleeves rolled up to his forearms, and he looked movie-star *hot*.

"Wow," he said, blinking as he took in her appearance. "Will we even look this good at the senior prom?"

She laughed. She loved his sense of humour.

"I didn't see you in the theatre," she said. How could she have possibly missed him?

"My dad snuck in the back," he said. "We're up in the last row. He's wearing a disguise. He looks just like that pic on the back of the *Club Weirdo* DVD."

Tori snickered. "Yeah right."

"Okay. That's a lie. But we *are* hiding in the back row." He checked his watch. "I'm supposed to meet him in the projection room in a few minutes. He's signing autographs for the theatre people and then we have to leave."

"Oh, that's too bad," she said. "You'll miss the rest of the movie."

"We'll catch it sooner or later," he said. "We can get a copy for home or just see it on TV." Then he cleared his throat.

"How have you been all week?" he asked her; then before she could answer, he said, "Tori, tell me the truth. Are you avoiding me?"

"Um." She wanted to die. She had no idea what to say. "I don't want to," she blurted, then winced because that sounded so...so true.

"I don't want to," she continued, taking a deep breath. "But my dad says your dad is a client, so..."

"Oh." Michael exhaled, rolling back his eyes. "I'm *so* relieved! I thought you thought I had bad breath or something. But your *dad* thinks I have bad breath."

She laughed harder at his witty comeback. Every bone in her body felt like it was loosening up.

Before she could stop herself, she said, "He said I was too young for..." Warning bells went off. *Shut up. Don't go there.*

"For?" he prompted. When she blushed and gave her head a little shake, he said, "For going out with a boy?"

Going out? This was beyond rollerblading! Her heart was pounding so hard she was certain he could hear it.

She stared at him, unable once again to make friends with those pesky English syllables.

"Tori?" he said. "Is that what you were going to say?"

"The movie," she said, avoiding answering. "I'm supposed to be, um..."

"Or that you're too young...for a boyfriend?" Now *he* was blushing. He looked away and said, "Because I think it would be cool to be your boyfriend, Tori."

You do? she nearly cried. *You really, really do?*

She wanted to jump up and down and scream and laugh and throw her arms around him and – and—

"I have to go!" she nearly shouted, her brain finally reconnecting to her mouth. Shocked at how loudly and firmly she had said it, she lowered her voice. "My parents are here and we're sitting with Kallista's family." She *had* to discuss this with Kallista!

"Okay," Michael said. He took a breath. His cheeks were even redder, and he looked unsure of himself as he said in a rush, "Listen, Mark Durgan is having a party on Friday night. At his house. Live band. Meet me there?" He wrinkled his nose and added, with a lopsided smile, "That way, it won't be a date and your dad can't not let you go."

A date that wasn't a date! "Oh, I—"

"Kallista's invited too, of course," he said. "It's pretty much an open party."

He was making it very hard to say no. And why should she say no? It was just a party! It wasn't a date!

"I...I'll see," she said, even though she wanted to shout, "Yes, yes, yes!" just like in the shampoo commercial.

"I'll e-mail you the details," he told her. "It's going to be a good party. Live band," he said again. Maybe he didn't remember telling her that. Maybe he was that nervous, too. He sure seemed nervous.

"Cool," she said, then realized that she had just ended the no-e-mailing sitch with him. Her dad wouldn't like it if he knew. Or so she assumed. She didn't actually know what was okay and what wasn't. But despite what Michael had just said, she *did* know that meeting him at a party definitely wouldn't be okay with her dad.

But it's just because my dad doesn't know him, she thought, as she turned to go. *He would never, like, spill our family secrets to a magazine. Besides, we don't even have any family secrets!*

He walked with her, and she got a little anxious. What if her dad saw them come back in together? Would he think she had snuck out to see him?

As they came to the theatre door, he said, "I'll wait out here for my dad."

"I'm still sorry you're going to miss the end of the movie," she said, terribly relieved that he wasn't going back into the theatre.

"Yeah, well," he said, dropping his voice, "I'm not missing anything *important*."

Her skin prickled from the top of her head to her toes. "It was neat to run into you," she said.

He chuckled and reached forward to open the door for her. "Yeah, funny coincidence," he replied.

"Yeah, ha-ha, how funny," she said, laughing weakly. Then she went inside and scanned the flickering darkness for her parents. As she spotted them, she started up the carpeted stairs.

I saw Michael! I saw Michael and—

Wait a minute, she thought, as the guy on the end of their roped-off VIP row – could it be Heath Ledger? – rose so she could scoot past him. *Was Michael trying to tell me that it wasn't a coincidence that he ran into me out there? That maybe he was even* waiting *for me?*

Could that be any cooler?

She was overheating with joy.

As she sat down next to Kallista, her BFF whispered, "Are you okay? You were gone *for ever*."

"I'm great," she whispered back. "Kallista, I am *so* great!"

"What is *up* with you?" Kallista half-whispered, half-cried, and it was clear that she had figured out that Tori had good gossip. As she got shushed, Kallista giggled and whispered, "Have we got to talk?"

"Oh, yeah," Tori replied. "We have *so* got to talk!"

Valerie called her mom to tell her about her promotion to the advanced class. Her mom was happy for her. Then Valerie waited up really, really late until her dad came home from work to tell him. He was delighted – and even more so when she told him about the recital on Saturday for Ashanti Utu.

"That'll be something nice to look forward to," he told her as they walked together towards the kitchen. "I have a big presentation on Friday. That's why I'm putting in all these extra hours. So it'll be nice to watch your recital on Saturday to celebrate."

"Manzuma hasn't picked the dances yet," Valerie reminded him. "She might not pick mine."

"Oh, I can't believe that," he said, giving her a hug. "You're so good at everything you do, honey."

She hugged him back. Then Valerie's stepmother, Sharin, came out of the office she shared with Valerie's father. She was carrying a file folder and her reading glasses were perched on the crown of her head.

Sharin gave Valerie's dad a kiss and said, "Hi, honey.

Did you hear the good news about Valerie and LaToya?"

"Yes," he said.

Valerie caught herself before she pointed out that LaToya hadn't actually *had* any good news. She and she alone was the good-news-haver. Instead, she said, "I think I'd like to continue taking dance after Mom gets home. Do you think that would be okay?"

Her father considered. "Well, we'll have to discuss the tuition. LaToya is able to help out at the school for a discount."

"Maybe Mom could help pay for mine," she said. "Or there's this guy who answers the phone. LaToya used to do that. Maybe I could do that, too."

"That's possible." He smiled at her. Her stepmother did, too. "Both those sound like good ideas." He gave her a noogie. "You're really using your noggin."

Despite the noogie, she basked in his praise. Then, as the three of them walked into the kitchen, Valerie murmured, "Oops."

There were dishes all over the counters. Dirty dishes. Dishes with caked-on mashed potatoes and congealed gravy. And it was her turn tonight to do them.

"I'm sorry," she said, as the two adults turned to look at her. "I forgot."

"Understandable, with the good news and all," her

father said. But her stepmother didn't say anything. She just looked irritated.

"I'll get to them right now." Val rushed to the sink and turned on the water.

"Good idea," Sharin put in, her voice a little edgy. Valerie winced. Sharin was very big on chores, and especially on chores getting done on time. Valerie and her mom were both much more casual about such things, and sometimes when Val was at her dad's, she forgot that it was such a big deal to some people.

"Did you give Mr. Bubbles his medicine?" Sharin continued.

Valerie shut her eyes. She had not. And at the sound of his name, Mr. Bubbles rose from his bed in the adjoining laundry room and skittered on his toenails across the slippery tile floor.

Mr. Bubbles was the family pet, and Valerie used that term loosely. He was a pug, and his face was so smushed that she thought he looked like some weird alien creature. He also had a skin condition. Pieces of skin flaked off his sides and the top of his head, which she thought was unbelievably disgusting, and he had to be given pills for it, which was even more disgusting – you had to force his mouth open and push them down his throat.

"I'll give Mr. Bubbles his medicine after I do the

dishes," Valerie promised, pushing up the sleeves of her pyjamas.

Valerie yawned sleepily as she picked up the dish sponge. She wished Sharin had reminded her about the dishes. Or that LaToya had. While LaToya had done her homework, she had gone into the kitchen at least twice for snacks. That meant that she had seen the dishes and not said a word.

Thanks, LaToya, she thought.

CHAPTER EIGHT

By the time Valerie was finished with the dishes, the house was quiet, and she was exhausted. She went to use the bathroom and found that her dance clothes, which she had hand washed and hung in the shower to dry, were soaking wet. Probably from when LaToya had taken a shower, and not bothered to move them.

Thanks, LaToya.

She wrung them out and rehung them. Then she crawled into bed and dropped off immediately to sleep.

After the movie premiere, Tori put on her pink pyjamas with the black Eiffel Towers and French poodles and checked her e-mail. She saw Michael's name and her stomach did a little flip. She clicked open the message.

To: Tori
From: MichaelS
Subject: Party

Hey, Tori,

It was so great to see you 2nite. I didn't know if you knew Mark's address. It's 2123 Beverly Rancho Drive. Also, here's my cell: 310-555-2931. What's yours?
— Michael

Tori read the message over and over. She wished he had signed it, "Love, Michael". Or even with some Xs and Os. But it was too soon for something like that. The only guy who had ever signed a letter with "love" was her father. Still, it would have been so exciting!

What should she do? She really, really liked Michael. *Really*. But her dad had been very clear about her not hanging out with him, and meeting him at a party was definitely hanging out. She had told Kallista about it at the theatre, and Kallista definitely wanted to go to the party. But Tori just didn't know.

She had three days to decide. And luckily, she had her camp friends to help her make the decision.

* * *

To: Alyssa
From: Tori
Subject: Date?

Hi, Lyss,

You know that pic I sent you of my friends and me in our FREE ALYSSA T-shirts? Well, that is Cameron Stevenson's son and I'm totally crushing on him. And he likes me, too!

Here's the problem: his dad is a client of my dad's, and so my dad has told me not to hang out with him. Michael wants me to meet him at a party on Friday and I totally want to go! But what should I do about my dad?

Your friend,

Tori

Sitting in her jammies in her bedroom, Alyssa read the e-mail from Tori. Her mind immediately jumped to *Romeo and Juliet* – star-crossed lovers forbidden to be together.

Whoa! Alyssa thought, as inspiration struck. She opened up the jpeg of Tori, Michael and Tori's bud Kallista for inspiration.

She started sketching Tori and Michael as Romeo and Juliet, trying out different poses and even different outfits, until she finally settled on a velvet gown for Tori, and a blousy shirt and leggings for Michael.

She posed them beneath an arch of roses, imagining them meeting in secret. Maybe they were getting married! She saw them silent, and statue-still, on the brink of their great romantic tragedy. The whole idea gave her the shivers – in a good way.

Inspiration had struck again!

"Val?" her father called the next morning. "We have to go in ten minutes."

"Be there in five," she sang out.

LaToya was gliding down the hall, nibbling on a piece of toast. She walked on by, then returned.

She said, "Did you give the dog his medicine last night?"

Valerie thought a minute. Had she? She must have. "Yes," she said.

"Oh. Really? Because I accidentally moved his pills into my medicine cabinet yesterday afternoon, and they're still there." LaToya looked into the hall as if she were talking to someone else.

She was: Sharin stepped into the doorway. She was dressed for work in a black pinstriped suit.

"Valerie," she said angrily, "we don't lie in this house.

If Mr. Bubbles doesn't get his medicine, his condition could worsen."

"I didn't mean to—" Valerie began.

"Your father and I are going to have to have a talk with you about this," Sharin said.

Valerie tried again. "I'm sorry. I was just confused. I wasn't trying to lie to you."

"We'll discuss it later. Your father is waiting to drive you two girls to school."

Sharin left the room. Valerie heard Sharin's heels click down the hall. She glared at LaToya and said, "You planned that! You made sure she was there when you asked me about the medicine!"

LaToya just smiled.

Ten minutes later, she, her father and LaToya were on their way to school. Her father said, "Your stepmother told me about what happened this morning, Val. If you can't take your responsibilities more seriously, we may have to skip those dance lessons."

"Daddy!" she cried. Then her eyes ticked in the rear-view mirror to LaToya, who was *still* smiling.

"Mr. Bubbles is on a strict regimen," her father continued. "He has to get his medicine every day or he won't get better. Forgetting was bad enough, but it would have been much better if you had owned up to it."

She said, "Daddy, I thought I had given it to him. I won't mess up again. *Please* don't take away my lessons!"

In the back, LaToya leaned her head back and calmly closed her eyes as if to say, *My work here is done.*

Valerie was completely freaked. Her author report on Laura Ingalls Wilder was missing.

"It was here. In my folder," Valerie told her history teacher, Ms. Meyers.

"You know my policy," Ms. Meyers said. "People who don't turn in their homework get detention."

No! If she got detention, she would miss the carpool. And dance class. And LaToya knew that.

Would LaToya actually take my homework?

She said, "Please, Ms. Meyers. Something... happened to it. It was in my folder. Really." She took a deep breath. "I can tell you what I wrote. My paper was on Laura Ingalls Wilder. She was born in 1867 in Wisconsin."

The last bell of the day went off and Valerie jerked her head towards the door. She couldn't be late!

She rattled on, "She started writing when she was sixty. She tried to sell an autobiography but it was rejected. So she reworked the story and sold it as *Little House in the Big Woods.*"

"Go on," Ms. Meyers said.

"Um, she became a schoolteacher, to help pay for her sister to go to blind school."

"What was her sister's name?" Ms. Meyers asked.

I have to go! Valerie thought frantically.

"Mary," she said.

The teacher sighed. "All right. I'll let it go this time. You've always been a good student, so I'll give you the benefit of the doubt. But don't let it happen again."

"Thank you, so much," Valerie said, hurrying out of the room to get to her locker, then out to the kerb to wait for Mrs. Wilcox.

Her evil stepsister was already there, and so was the white Odyssey. Did LaToya looked surprised to see her? Valerie couldn't tell.

Mrs. Wilcox beeped her horn as Danielle threw open the van door and cried, "Hurry, you guys! My mom has a dentist appointment!"

"I'm telling Mom you kept us waiting," LaToya said to Valerie as she climbed into the passenger area. "Next time you're late, I'm going to tell them to leave without you."

Note to self, Valerie thought, *do not be late tomorrow, no matter what!*

*   *   *

They got to the studio. Valerie noticed that Antoine wasn't at his desk. LaToya noticed her noticing and said, "Antoine stole your homework and left the country."

"Ha ha," Valerie said. LaToya was sticking to her story that she hadn't gone anywhere near Valerie's report on Laura Ingalls Wilder.

"Actually, he quit," LaToya said.

Maybe I could have his job, she thought. *If I can pay for my classes, maybe I won't have to quit. Maybe paying for them can be my consequences for lying.*

There was a big sign tacked on the wall next to the poster of Alvin Ailey. It read, *"There will be no beginners' class tomorrow. The studio will close early in preparation for the recital to honour Ashanti Utu on Saturday at 10 a.m."*

They quickly changed and warmed up. Then Manzuma gave them the rest of the class time to work on their dances.

"I'm doing a poem, like you," one of the other girls told Valerie.

"Me, too!" said the girl who usually wore China blue.

Valerie was shocked. It seemed that half the students were copying her idea by using steps to stand for words in poems and even song lyrics. Four of them were dancing together, and there were two sets of three girls.

146

And their dances were more elaborate and complicated than hers.

Even LaToya was one of the copiers. "Like it?" she asked Valerie. "I'm using a poem by Maya Angelou. Manzuma loves Maya Angelou's work." The nerve! Especially after warning Valerie not to get too excited about the audition. The worst part was that LT's dance was really beautiful.

This is terrible, Valerie thought. *I can't compete with these girls. They're all better dancers than I am.*

And no one else – including Manzuma – seemed to notice or care that everyone was stealing her idea. All Manzuma said to her was, "Tomorrow is the big day!"

To: Jenna
From: Valerie
Subject: My evil stepsister!

Dear Jenna,

LT is doing all these mean things to me! I think she's trying to make sure I can't try out for the recital. I am in such big trouble with my dad & stepmom that I don't think they would listen if I tried to tell them about it.

Now she is stealing my dance idea! Half the class is doing dance poems now!

What should I do?

KIT,

Valerie

To: Valerie

From: Jenna

Subject: LT

Dear Val,

I am so sorry! Try to remember that she is doing these things because she is worried you will take one of the four spots in the recital. Which must mean she is threatened by you! And she has been dancing for YEARS! So you must be a good dancer. Maybe your parents WILL listen. Try to do everything extra right until the audition, okay?

And that is YOUR idea and your teacher knows that. So she probably thinks you are a genius.

Hang in! Stay strong!

Your CLF,

Jenna

*   *   *

On Friday, Alyssa woke up two hours earlier than usual. She turned on the light and stared down at her portrait of Tori and Michael. They stood carefully posed beneath the rose arch, Romeo and Juliet getting married.

A slow smile spread across her face. It was really, really good.

But something was bothering her. She wasn't sure what it was. Was she worried about what would happen if she tried to submit another contest entry? *Not really.* There had been no more protesting at school, and she and Mr. Prescott had had a good week. Things seemed to be back to normal.

And this picture is really good. But still...

Still what? She didn't know.

She carefully placed it into her black leather portfolio and got ready for school. When Beckah and Rose showed up, they saw the portfolio, and Beckah whooped.

"You did another piece! Let us see it!" she demanded.

"I want to hurry to school, so I can show it to Mr. Prescott before first period," she told them.

The three friends got to school with fifteen minutes to spare, and they headed straight for the art room. Mr. Prescott was at his desk. There was a large stack of drawings and sketches on top of all his other stacks of stuff. Contest entries.

She drew in her breath as he turned his head and smiled. He saw the portfolio and said, "Back again? Good for you."

She hesitated. Then she walked to his desk with her portfolio in her arms. Beckah and Rose tiptoed behind her. Her heart pounded as she pulled out her sketch and handed it to him.

"Oh." He studied her work. "Alyssa, what a surprise." He smiled at her. "You have quite a flair for portraiture."

A thrill shot up her spine. *Yes!*

"Flowers, maybe not so much," she ventured.

He smiled. "Still life may not be your thing. You're about people."

And that was when Alyssa knew what was wrong.

She said, "When's the deadline for submissions?"

"Today at noon," he replied. "Why? This is perfectly fine. I'll log it in and—"

Noon. She had classes straight through until twelve thirty.

She took another deep breath and shook her head. "No, Mr. Prescott. I don't want to enter this picture."

Beckah and Rose stared at her.

"Are you nuts?" Beckah cried.

Alyssa's eyes welled as she picked up the picture. Maybe it was "perfectly fine", but...

"It's not my best," she said.

It's Friday, Valerie thought as she climbed into the Camry. The day Manzuma would select the dances for the recital.

Valerie hadn't slept a wink the night before, and when she climbed into the Camry in the morning, her father said, "I think you should know we haven't decided if you can continue taking dance lessons after your mom comes home. Sharin's very disappointed with you over what happened with Mr. Bubbles, and I agree with her, Val. What you did should have consequences. But for today..."

He smiled at her. "Break a leg. Both you girls."

"Thank you, Daddy," Val said breathlessly.

LaToya just glared at Valerie and put her iPod plugs in her ears.

Posted by: Priya
Subject: Smoothie Town Grand Opening!

Hi, Double-Bunk Bloggers,

Tonight my mom is opening her smoothie bar. She is way stressed out and I have to admit that I am, too. My new lab partner is totally focused on winning the Tri-County Regional Science Fair. Leslie wants us to work on it 24/7. I only wanted to do a project that was good enough to enter, and I don't want to work on it all the time. But I don't know how to tell her.

Plus, there is this cute boy named Riley. He works at his uncle's hot dog stand in the food court and he goes to my school. He wanted to have lunch with me on Monday, but I had to work on the science fair project with Leslie. He came by my locker two other times but – yep, you guessed it – I had to go work on the project.

Meanwhile, it looks like Jordan must have come up with a good experiment because he stops by Ms. Romero's desk a lot and she is always laughing with him. I remember when I used to laugh with him.

I am so confused about what is happening.

Anyway, please wish the Shahs luck on the opening of Smoothie Town!

Your CLF,

Priya

Posted by: Alex
Subject: Re: Smoothie Town Grand Opening!

Dear Priya,

I am so sorry you are stressed out. Maybe you can tell Leslie you want to have lunch with Riley today and that you will work on the project this weekend. It sounds like you will be very busy with helping your mom and the project, so maybe you can reward yourself with some "Riley time" at lunch?

I hope everyone is doing well. I'm doing well in soccer and my diabetes is under control. So no complaints here.

Your friend,
Alex

CHAPTER NINE

Priya dawdled in the morning, reading Alex's Camp Lakeview blog posting, so she had barely scooted inside her first period classroom when the bell rang. What Alex had written made perfect sense.

I'm going to do it, she said. *I'm going to tell Leslie I'm having lunch with Riley today. I have worked really hard on that project for a whole week and I deserve some time off.*

She was both excited and nervous about her decision, and she caught herself silently practising what she would say all morning. By the time the lunch bell rang, she felt like she had actually had her conversation with Leslie.

So when Leslie came up to her at the doorway to the cafeteria and said, "I've got our table," Priya's response was very well rehearsed.

"Um, I'm sorry, Leslie," she said, suddenly very nervous. *What was I going to say? Oh, yeah!*

"I don't want to work on the project at lunch today. I need a break."

Leslie's eyes grew huge. Her mouth dropped open. She gave her head a little shake as if she just *knew* she hadn't heard Priya correctly.

"*What?*"

Priya cleared her throat. "I'm buying my lunch, too," she said. Which was kind of necessary, as she had used up all the bread and peanut butter in the house.

Leslie just stared her. Priya got even more nervous. Then Leslie said, "I have done ninety per cent of all the work on this project, and you can't even help this little bit?"

"Leslie, all I do is work on this project," Priya said. "I'm not even doing all my homework. And my mom needs me. My brother broke his leg and he can't help her."

"Well, you can't help her at lunch," Leslie argued. "Are you going to do your homework instead of helping me?"

Priya took a breath. "No," she said. "I'm – I'm going to eat my lunch with Riley."

"Oh, really?" Leslie asked. "Does *she* know that?"

She pointed to the lunch line. Priya turned, looked, and felt her heart crack right down the middle.

The laughing red-headed girl from Riley's lunch

table was standing in front of him in line. They were practically touching, and he was gazing down at her with a warm, happy smile. They were in a bubble of togetherness, and everyone else in line was leaving them alone.

"Oh, no," Priya murmured, stricken. Had she imagined that he was liking her? No. He had asked her to have lunch with him. More than once.

And she had said no each time.

Had he given up on her?

Taking a deep breath, she turned back to Leslie. "Well," she said, "I guess I can work on the project after all."

Leslie raised her chin. "No, you can't," she informed her. "You're weighing me down, Shah. I don't want you to be my partner any more."

She whirled around and stomped away.

"Leslie, wait!" Priya called. She started to follow her, then stopped. She didn't know what to do next. Was Leslie actually kicking her off her project? Could she do that?

Why not? I did it. I kicked Jordan off.

Then the double doors to the kitchen opened, and Jordan breezed out in his silly hairnet and apron. This time, he was carrying an entire tray of metal dishes.

In front of Jordan, Riley and the girl were moving

through the food line, laughing and talking. Then she reached up and touched his cheek.

Priya's whole body felt like crying. Her eyes welled. Everything was going wrong, all at once.

To her horror, she did begin to cry.

Even worse, Jordan saw it.

Covering her face, Priya bolted out of the cafeteria.

Valerie got through the day on sheer adrenalin.

The dismissal bell finally rang. Valerie hustled to her locker and arranged everything in her backpack, making sure her nice, dry, clean dance clothes were in it.

"Hey, Val." It was Shaneece. "Today's your big day, right?"

Valerie wrinkled her nose. "Yes. I'm feeling a little nervous."

"You're gonna kick it, girl!" Shaneece insisted. She held up her hand. "High five, woman!"

Valerie laughed and high-fived her friend's open palm. The words of encouragement were exactly what she needed.

"Okay, I'm kicking it," she told Shaneece.

She moved into the bustle of the crowd and brisked around the same corner LaToya had taken. Lots of kids were headed towards the pick-up area, and as she walked along with them, she mentally went through her dance steps. It was too late to change her idea and come up with something different. Her only hope was that she would do her best, and that her best would be good enough.

She got to the flagpole and scanned the parade of cars as she looked around for LaToya. And after a few minutes of standing around waiting, Valerie realized that Mrs. Wilcox's white Odyssey was nowhere to be seen.

She checked her watch. They should have been here by now. Her stomach started to clench. She licked her lips.

"Hey, you're LaToya's stepsister. Are you looking for her?" asked a tall boy in a dark blue pea coat. When Valerie nodded eagerly he said, "She left about ten minutes ago. In that white van that always picks her up."

Valerie stared at him. She felt faint. *"What?"*

"Yeah. She came running out of the school, waving her arms at them. She jumped right in and they took off in a big hurry."

He smiled at Valerie and trotted off.

Valerie was swaying in shock. LaToya had ditched her so that she would miss their dance class.

I am not missing that audition, she thought.

* * *

Mr. Prescott was nibbling on a protein bar in his left hand while he graded papers — art history quizzes, Alyssa guessed — with his right hand.

"You wanted to see me?" she asked, hovering in the doorway.

"Alyssa, hi, yes," he said, gesturing for her to come on in. "Thanks for stopping by. I felt that we had more to talk about this morning, but we didn't get a chance." He put down his pencil and protein bar and folded his hands on his desk. "I'm curious why you didn't want to enter *Romeo and Juliet* in the contest."

"I told you," she said, as she drew near his desk. When he stayed silent, as if waiting for her to continue, she hesitated, and then she began.

"I realized that I want to draw people."

"Portraiture," he said.

She shook her head. "People in motion. People who are dancing, or laughing, or arguing. People who are living. When you said I wasn't into 'still life', you were talking about *Roses at Dawn*. But then I realized that *Romeo and Juliet* is just as much of a still life as those flowers. That's not interesting to me."

"Wow." Mr. Prescott's eyes widened. Then his mouth stretched into the widest smile she had ever seen on his face. It nearly split his face in two.

"Wow," he said again, more softly. "I have just

watched an artist discover her style. Alyssa, this is wonderful."

"It...is?" she asked in a small voice. But she could feel herself catching some of his excitement.

He nodded. "You know that in class we've talked about people who enjoy doing art."

"The Sunday dabblers," she said.

He smiled. "Yes. The Sunday dabblers. They paint a seascape because they like the ocean. Or sketch a vase of flowers because they don't know what else to draw and they know that lots of artists sketch flowers. They're seeing with their eyes. That's enough for them. And that's just fine. Art works on many different levels."

"Yes," Alyssa said, following him.

"But *you've* discovered how to see with your creative spirit. You were seized with inspiration when you created *Ode to a Woman*. Then, when I rejected it, you tried to dabble by painting the flowers. But you couldn't just paint to paint something."

"That's true," she said. That was it exactly. She had painted the flowers because she didn't know what else to paint.

"So you tried again," he said. "You got closer to your true vision this time, because you returned to people as your subject. And you chose subjects near to your heart. I'm assuming the couple are people you know."

160

She nodded.

"But the posed couple was not 'your' people as they truly are." He made air quotes. "Your people move. Breathe. Live." He smiled again at her.

"Yes," she said. "I knew that was why it was wrong."

"This entire creative struggle has matured you as an artist, Alyssa. You knew that it wasn't enough for you to paint something just to win the *Works* contest."

"Right," she replied steadily. "I want to do my art to learn about who I am. And then to share who I am... through my art."

He beamed at her. "You will. I have no doubt of that."

"Thank you, Mr. Prescott," she said. She was all choked up.

"I've been thinking about *Ode*. It's still wrong for the contest," he said quickly. "But I think it's worth sharing."

"You do?"

He nodded. "So do other people. Principal Caya saw it on the Net. There are a couple of galleries in town that might like to see it. One is owned by a group of artists who are always looking for exciting new work. The other specializes in art by women. I'll write down the names for you."

Alyssa chest was tight. She was dazed. She nodded and tried to say "Thank you," but she couldn't speak.

Instead she ducked her head, turned around, and walked out the door.

Valerie was freaking out. She called her dad on her cellphone and told him what had happened – that LaToya had gotten the carpool to ditch her and now she would miss her chance to try out for the recital!

"Please come and get me," she begged.

"I can't, sweetie," he told her. "I'm in the middle of *my* big presentation. I can't leave."

"What am I going to do?" she wailed.

"Can you call the school and explain? Maybe your teacher can make other arrangements for you to audition."

"Yes!" she cried. "I'll call right away!"

She punched in the number, but the phone rang and rang. With Antoine gone, it seemed that no one was answering the phone! She kept waiting for the message system to kick in, but nothing happened.

Now she was even more freaked out! She was just about to call her father back when her cellphone rang, playing an Alicia Keys download.

"Daddy?" she said.

"Hi." It was Sharin. "Your dad said you missed the van."

"It left without me!" she protested. "I went right outside." She started to lose it. "Sharin, I'm sorry I lied to you about the dog, but I am not lying to you now. LaToya made them leave without me, because today is the day we find out who gets to dance at the recital tomorrow!"

"That's a harsh accusation," Sharin observed.

She'll never believe me, Valerie thought sadly. *She'll just think I'm talking trash about her precious daughter.*

"I know it's harsh, but it's true. I called the school to tell them, but the phone just rings and rings. I – I don't know what to do." She started to cry. She didn't want to cry on the phone with her stepmother, but she couldn't help it.

There was a long pause. Valerie could hear her heart thundering. Then Sharin said, "I'm in the middle of a very important meeting."

So is everyone else, Valerie thought, despairing.

"I'd suggest a cab, but the service in our town is so unreliable," Sharin continued.

Valerie heard her sigh. Then Sharin said, "Okay, listen. I'm coming for you, Valerie. Hang on. I'll be there."

Valerie was stunned. Her stepmother – the person who was threatening to take away her dance lessons – was leaving work for *her*?

"Thank you," Valerie said in a rush. "Thank you so much!"

"I'll be there soon. Just wait for me."

"I'll wait," Valerie said.

It was Friday afternoon, and Tori had gotten permission to spend the night at Kallista's. She was *soooo* relieved. Her parents had never said no, but she was feeling superstitious. It all seemed just a little too good to be true.

She packed a sparkly top and a pair of what she and Kallista called "kitten shoes" – little backless heels – and about thirty different make-up samples her mom had given her. She'd kissed her parents goodnight and then she and Kallista went home with Kallista's older cousin, Mischa. After working on their look for an hour or so in Kallista's bathroom with the special make-up mirror, Mischa drove them through the tree-lined boulevards of Beverly Hills with the top down. So much for their hair!

"Alyssa sent me the coolest pic," Tori told them. "It's me and Michael dressed up like Romeo and Juliet."

"Romeo and Juliet first met at a party," Mischa said.

"Forbidden love is so romantic," Kallista cooed, grinning at Tori.

Forbidden is right. I am going against everything my dad told me, she thought as she smiled back at Kallista.

Glammed and glittered, Mischa and Kallista scampered through Mark Durgan's giganto mansion to the backyard, where the party was in full swing. Tori followed behind, beyond excited, but also feeling even more guilty.

The live band was jammin' on the opposite side of the enormous swimming pool. There were tons of kids Tori recognized from school, tons of other kids she didn't...and—

"Parents!" Tori cried.

There were grown-ups *everywhere*. As the three girls gaped in astonishment, one of them caught sight of Tori and gave her a wave. It was Cameron Stevenson. His wife, Elise, was next to him. And next to her...Romeo!

Michael was adorable in black jeans, boots and a nice white T-shirt. He was biting down on a breadstick. When he turned and saw Tori, he beamed and waved the breadstick at her.

"Wow! He's glowing like a light bulb!" Kallista said, giggling.

Michael headed straight for the three girls. Tori's stomach filled with butterflies and her brain filled with empty blank spaces.

"Michael!" Kallista cried. "We didn't know parents were invited."

Michael's Pacific blue eyes gleamed as he quirked a half-grin at Tori. "I kind of figured that if I told you that you could invite your parents, they'd know about the party. And if they knew about the party, your dad wouldn't let you come."

Tori nodded. Good strategy. But hearing it made her guilt double.

"I'm glad you came," he said. His voice was low and there was pink in his cheeks.

"Me too," she said as she felt her face get hot, and wondered if she was blushing, too.

At least, ninety-eight per cent of me.

CHAPTER TEN

Priya made up a bogus excuse about feeling sick and got sent home at lunch.

Her mother said, "You got out of school so you could help me, didn't you."

"Hmm," Priya answered, not wanting to lie but for sure not wanting to tell her what had happened. This close to the grand opening, it was way too much to go into.

She spent a couple of hours helping her mom load the van up. Sam hobbled out to the kerb and Priya helped him in. Then the three of them drove to Smoothie Town. Priya's dad was coming a little later.

Priya helped her mother set up and make some smoothie samples. Sam did what he could, given his crutches. Then they loaded a batch into small plastic sample cups on the baby blue plastic tray from home. The original plan had been for Priya and Sam to wander the mall, passing out samples, but now it would just be Priya.

Mr. Simpson came by with a vase of red roses and a card decorated with popping champagne bottles and fireworks that said, CONGRATULATIONS! YOU DID IT!

He and Riley had signed it. Priya stared down at Riley's handwriting and swallowed down her sadness. Okay, lunch had been bad. But for all she knew, he didn't really like that other girl.

Right.

"This is so kind of you," Priya's mother told Mr. Simpson. "Is Riley going to work tonight? I'd like to thank him for helping us out."

"Yes, he'll be here in a bit," Mr. Simpson said. "He enjoyed helping you. Maybe sometimes just a little too much." He gave Priya a friendly wink.

Priya tried to smile back, but her mouth was on strike and she gave up the effort. She took the tray and said, "I'll pass out samples now."

"Thank you, honey." Her mother took a deep breath.

"Wish me luck, Mom," she said.

She walked to the entrance of the food court and called out, "Free samples from Smoothie Town! Grand opening at Smoothie Town!"

People in coats and hats just wandered past. A little

girl darted over to her, grabbed a cup, glanced up at Priya, and took another.

She said, "These are the perfect size for my Barbies." Then she scooted away.

"Free samples," Priya said.

A middle-aged man in a thick down jacket came over and said, "Young lady, do you know where the sporting goods store is?"

"Just down this side of the mall," she replied. "Would you like a free sample?"

He looked down at the little cups of colourful smoothies, then back up at her.

He said, "No." Then he walked away.

Well, Priya thought. *This is not going so great.*

"Free samples," she called out weakly.

"Oh, for heaven's sake," a voice drawled. "You gotta sell it, girl!"

Jordan!

He was dressed in a white T-shirt, a tuxedo jacket, and a pair of jeans. He grabbed the tray from her and bellowed, "Free! Free! Free! The best smoothies in town! Totally free for the next ten minutes only! So get 'em now!"

Two girls, a blond and a brunette, giggled as they walked up. The blond one batted her lashes at him and said, "Did you make them?"

"Sure," he said. "And they are *excellent*." He jerked his head backwards. "Go to Smoothie Town and tell them Jordan sent you."

The blond sipped. "Oh, it *is* good," she said.

"Smoothie T-O-W-N," he said. "Go now."

"Okay, but we'll be back," the blond told him.

"Great." Then he bellowed, "Free smoothies!"

People started gathering around him and taking the samples. Before long the tray was empty.

He turned to Priya. "Okay, where were we?" he said, looking a little uncertain and shy.

"Oh, Jordan," she said.

And then she hugged him.

"I'm sorry," she said into his chest. "I really messed up. Leslie hates me and I lost Riley and everything is horrible."

"And don't forget — you and I made up. Which also must stink for you," he prompted.

She smiled. "I'm sorry. You have no idea how glad I am that we made up. I guess I assumed that was understood."

They began to walk back to Smoothie Town. Jordan said, "First of all, Leslie does not hate you, but she did ask Ms. Romero to take you off the project. She is joining forces with the great Marco, and I'm sure they will be very happy together."

"Oh, great," she groaned. "I'm getting a C."

He shook his head. "I asked Ms. Romero if you could be on *my* project." He wiggled his eyebrows. "My project that she *loves*. And she said yes."

She caught her lower lip and squinted up at him. "You would do that? After I dumped you?"

He whapped her with the tray again. "I don't know. Maybe not. You're pretty dense, Shah. You might not be any help at all."

"You really are a good friend." She wrinkled her nose. "I'm sorry I lost faith in you."

"You were right to," he said, shrugging. "I *was* all Brynn, Brynn, Brynn. But you know, not to start another fight – no way! – but you could have come up with a topic yourself."

She hadn't thought of that. He had a good point. "You're right. I could have."

"But it's a good thing that you didn't," he continued, "since *my* idea rocks the house!"

"What is your idea?" she asked. "What's the project?"

"How Things Rot," he said proudly. "I've been collecting rotting things all week. You cannot *believe* what goes on in the cafeteria garbage bins!"

She laughed. "*That's* why you've been in the kitchen in a hairnet?"

"No." He shook his head. "I've decided to follow my childhood dream of becoming a lunch lady."

"Oh, Jordan," she said fondly. "You are such a dork."

"No, I'm just your BFF," he replied. *"He's the dork."*

He pointed to Simpson's Hot Dogs. Riley was standing behind the counter in a navy blue turtleneck sweater and a great pair of jeans. He had gotten a haircut and he looked fabulous.

And Miss Lunch Line was standing on the other side of the counter, leaning on her forearms and flirting with him. Red hair, brown eyes, gorgeous lacy top and all.

"C'mere," Jordan said, grabbing Priya's wrist. He started walking towards the hot dog counter.

"No, J!" Priya begged, grabbing at her wrist. "Let go of me!"

He kept walking. Riley turned his head to look at them. Priya dropped her hand away from Jordan's wrist so she wouldn't make a scene, but she pretty much wanted to die.

They kept walking. Riley kept looking. Her face was blazing hot and she seriously needed to remember how to breathe.

"Hey, Riley," Jordan said, all cheery. "I'm here for my grease."

"Cool." Riley glanced at Priya. She couldn't read his expression. He had a different stud in his ear. He looked great in navy blue. She wanted him to like her again. She wanted things to be great between them.

"Priya," he said. "I went over to your mom's stand to wish you guys good luck. You weren't there, so I figured you were working on your project with Leslie."

"Ms. Shah has joined my team," Jordan informed him. "She realized that my project is superior, and she also wanted a life."

Riley smiled at Priya.

Priya's sun came out.

The girl in front of the counter blurted, "See? I told you it would work out!" Then she covered her mouth and laughed. "Oops!"

Riley blinked, looking flustered as he said, "This is Marta, my..."

"I'm his...advisor," Marta told Priya. "On certain matters. Named Priya."

As Riley got even more flustered, Marta giggled and said, "I'll go now. Jay's waiting." She added, "Jay's my boyfriend."

Jordan said, "I'll go get my rotting hot dogs. Priya, you are going to love congealed meat grease. It *rots* the house."

He ducked under the counter, leaving Riley and Priya as alone as two people could be in a food court on a late Friday afternoon. He smelled so good. He looked so happy.

"Hi, again," Riley said.

And that was all he needed to say.

"C'mon, c'mon," Valerie pleaded. It was getting dark and she was cold. She kept checking the time on her cellphone. Class was nearly over!

She tried calling her dad but she got his voicemail.

She tried Sharin's number and Sharin answered.

"Valerie, I'm so sorry!" she cried. "I had a fender bender. We're exchanging information. I'm almost done."

"Okay," Valerie murmured. Even though it wasn't at all. It was horrible. Then she thought to ask, "Are you okay?"

"I'm fine. I'll be there soon."

Tears of frustration filled her eyes as she flipped her phone closed. She tried the studio over and over. *Still* no answer!

Then, just as Valerie was about to dissolve into a puddle of tears, Sharin screeched up beside her in her Sentra. The passenger-side front bumper was slightly dented. Valerie let out a whoop and jumped into the passenger seat.

"Valerie! I'm so sorry! What a horrible day!"

"I'm just glad you're okay," Valerie said in a small voice. She tried to smile at her stepmother, but she saw the digital readout of the time on the dashboard. There were only five minutes left to class.

"That is really sweet," Sharin told her.

Sharin drove fast. But as soon as they pulled up to the kerb in front of Fusion Space, Valerie knew it was too late. The lights in the front office were off.

Undaunted, Sharin marched up to the door and rang the bell. Valerie stood beside her. They waited. Valerie held her breath. But no one came to answer the door.

Her stepmother rang it again.

Nothing.

Sharin tried a third time. She pounded really hard on the door and bellowed, "Hello? Ms. Manzuma?"

And then...the lights came on. And the door opened.

Manzuma stood before them with a kimono wrapped around her slender frame. She looked both surprised and pleased to see Valerie.

"Valerie, we missed you!" she said. "What happened? LaToya said you missed your ride."

"I didn't," Valerie said in a rush. "She left without me. I tried to call..."

"Come in, come in," Manzuma said. She glanced over at the phone on Antoine's desk.

It was off the hook. Manzuma got a funny look on

her face as she put it back on the hook, then punched a few buttons.

"The message system has been turned off," she said. "I don't think that can happen by accident."

LaToya! Oh, she is so evil!

Valerie said in a halting voice, "Did you...did you pick the dances?"

Manzuma gazed at her with a sad expression. "Yes, I did. I picked four. And before you ask, yes, one of them was LaToya's. She created something quite exciting. She went in an entirely different direction from simply copying your idea. Which I was glad to see, I might add. So many of the others did just that – did variations on your new style."

"What new style?" Sharin asked. "I thought LaToya had invented some new kind of dance that *you* had tried to imitate. That's what she told me, anyway."

She would, Valerie thought bitterly.

"Where is LaToya?" Sharin asked. "She knows she's supposed to wait for me here."

"Well, she said she wasn't sure if you would remember there was no beginners' class today. It was cancelled because of the recital. She said you had an important meeting at work. So she got a ride home with Linda."

"She is in so much trouble," Sharin muttered. "She

never even mentioned that there was no beginners' class today."

"Maybe I should have told you," Valerie said. "I'm sorry."

"No," Sharin said. "You and I...were having some tension. But LaToya..." She trailed off. "LaToya and I are going to have a talk."

Wow! She's on my side! Valerie was *so* grateful.

Manzuma looked at Sharin and Valerie for a moment. "Valerie, why don't you dance one more time for me?"

Before Valerie could answer, Manzuma turned on the hall light and led the way into the dance room. Then she moved into the darkness. There was a hiss and the smell of a lighted match, and then she lit a candle. And another. And another. The walls of the dance room flickered with light. The dance room looked even more magical to Valerie than when the regular lights were on.

"Come and dance," Manzuma urged Valerie.

"I don't have on my dance clothes," Valerie said.

"The clothes a dancer dances in *are* her dance clothes," Manzuma replied.

"I'd like to see your dance," Sharin added.

Feeling shy, Valerie shucked off her heavy outerwear and her black boots. Then she did a few stretches while Manzuma crossed to the boom box and put in a disc.

Valerie assumed her opening position. Then the music swelled through her, filling her, and she began to move. She swooped and fell, rose and stretched. She glided. She leaped.

She *danced*.

She forgot about LaToya. She forgot about her stepmother. She even forgot about Manzuma. All she thought about was...

I
am
I am a
woman-to-be
a woman-to-be strong and free
I am
a body humming
a heart strumming
a spirit thrumming
changing, growing, becoming,
I
I am
I am a
woman now
I!

It was over before she was really ready for it to be over. She held her last position – which was the same as her first – as the music faded, then ended.

"Oh, Valerie," Sharin breathed. She began to applaud. Manzuma did, too.

Then a third pair of hands joined in.

Valerie dropped her pose and looked in the direction of the sound.

A tall, dark woman wearing a long black dress and silvery grey hair in a bun glided from the corner of the room towards Valerie. As she approached, she smiled and held out her arms.

"Ah, c'est belle," she said. "Your dance is beautiful."

"Valerie, this is Ashanti Utu," Manzuma said. "She arrived a few minutes ago, after the other students had already left. You're the first of my dancers to meet her."

Valerie's lips parted. The very woman she had hoped to show her moves to! And she, Valerie, had danced for her all alone!

"You have a gift," Ashanti said, enfolding Valerie in her arms. She pulled back slightly and studied Valerie's face. "Manzuma told me of your creation. Very interesting. Very lovely." She smiled at Sharin. "You must be so proud of your daughter."

"Thank you. I am." She smiled warmly at Valerie.

"Do I see you dance again tomorrow?" Ashanti asked.

Valerie looked at Manzuma, who smiled and nodded. "I'll make room for another dance," she said.

"That probably won't be necessary," Sharin said. "I'll give her the benefit of the doubt until I speak to her, but my guess is that LaToya will be home tomorrow while we're here. In other words, not performing."

"Ah." Manzuma looked sad. "LaToya didn't have to resort to underhanded tricks to get a place in the recital. She should have trusted her artistic instincts. Her new dance was very strong."

"It is never strong to win with tricks," Ashanti Utu said. She smiled at Valerie. "Remember that. You are a warrior of art."

I am a Zulu Warrior Dancer, Valerie thought giddily.

Tori tried to have fun. She ate some pizza and danced with Michael, Kallista and Mischa. She talked to a bunch of girls from school. But she was torn. If she was going to have to lie to her parents and sneak around to be with Michael, maybe...maybe she shouldn't do it.

"Hey," he said, with his blue eyes and his cute gap in his teeth and his friendliness and his everythingness. "This worked out pretty well, huh?"

She nodded, but her heart wasn't in it. She couldn't

tell if he noticed. He was nervous, too, but he was also very happy. Everything should have been perfect...but it wasn't.

Dancing to a wild beat, Kallista bobbed over to the two of them and said, "What's wrong?"

"Oh, Kallista, I'm just, um...*oh NO*," Tori said, staring past Kallista.

Her parents were there! And they were staring right at her!

"Oops, you're busted big-time," Kallista said. "Me, not so much, probably, because my parents would have been cool with the party. So if you die, can I have all your shoes?"

"Shut up," Tori said faintly.

Michael said, "I'm here, Tori. Which is probably the main problem." He frowned. "How did they know where you were?"

"No clue," Tori muttered. Then she licked her lips as her father and mother approached. They were both dressed casually, as if they'd planned to settle in for an evening home alone.

"Tori Ann!" her father began, stomping towards her. Then she knew she was in major trouble, because he never used her middle name.

"Easy, honey," her mother said to him.

"Hi, um, Daddy——" Tori began.

But she was interrupted by Michael's father as he and Michael's mother walked up.

"James, so glad you could make it," Cameron Stevenson said jovially to Tori's father. Tori couldn't tell if Mr. Stevenson realized that her father was mad. But the two men shook hands, and the moms smiled at each other. It was like a commercial in the middle of the movie of her tragic demise.

"Dad, you *called* Tori's parents?" Michael asked, his eyes wide.

It was obvious that his father didn't get that this was a problem. "Yeah. I saw Tori and that reminded me to ask about putting a clause in my contract about travel for the family. So I asked myself why they weren't here at this great party. I called them and told them how much fun we were all having. And here they are."

He smiled brightly at Tori's father. "I think you mentioned you wanted to get to know Al Durgan. He's got some great new data about residuals on cellphone downloads."

"Oh?" her father said. He pursed his lips. "I do want to talk to him. But first..." He looked hard at Tori.

Tori swallowed. "Um..."

Her dad said, "Let's walk." He took Tori's mom's hand. "Just the three of us."

"Okay," Tori said in a small voice. She tried to smile

at Michael, but she couldn't. Her heart was breaking into a million pieces. She knew her dad was going to ground her for life and tell her that she could never even look in Michael's direction again.

They walked down a path to a marble fountain of an angel pouring water out of a jar. Then the family of three stopped, and Tori's parents both gave her the bug eye.

"You lied to us," her father said. "You snuck out to see that boy. After I told you that you couldn't see him outside of school!"

"Oh, dear, why not?" Tori's mother asked, looking extremely worried. "He seems like such nice boy."

"He is," Tori got in. "But his dad is Cameron Stevenson, and he's a client. And it's the industry, and what if he gets interviewed and we don't *have* any family secrets, Daddy!" She could hear herself babbling, but she was so upset and nervous that she couldn't stop herself.

"Honey," Tori's mom said.

Both her husband and her daughter said, "Yes?"

And that broke the ice, somehow, that both of them were "honey". All three of them smiled at each other.

Tori decided to try again. "Look, you know that I bunked with Natalie Goode last summer."

Her parents both nodded.

"Well, she told me this story about this girl who pretended to be Natalie's friend, so her mom could get a part in her dad's next movie."

"O...kay," her dad said slowly.

"But her mom didn't get the part, and she got revenge by going to the tabloids and sharing confidential stuff Natalie had told her daughter."

"Oh, how awful," Tori's mother breathed. "I hate that kind of thing."

"That's my point," her dad said. "It's so hard to have normal relationships in this town."

"Natalie was just here for the summer," Tori pointed out. "She isn't around the industry 24/7, like me. *And* that happened when Natalie was a little kid. I'm in middle school!"

"Still, throw in the whole boy-girl thing, and it could be a huge fiasco."

Her mother said, "Tori sounds like she's aware that there may be pitfalls." She looked thoughtful and said, "This is what you were talking about when you asked me about movie people dating each other."

Tori nodded. "I'm sorry I didn't come right out and talk to you guys about it. I know it was wrong to sneak behind your back."

Her father scratched his head, the way he did when he was thinking hard about something. Tori stopped herself from babbling again, and gave him a chance to process their discussion so far. He was a lawyer; he thought things through.

"I didn't realize you felt so strongly about Michael," he began. "I was trying to warn you away before anything started."

"Well, it did already start," Tori confessed. "He's really nice, Daddy, and he even got a FREE ALYSSA T-shirt."

Her father smiled faintly. "Yes, he's nice. But you're also a warm-hearted girl who could get hurt."

"I promise never to get hurt," she said.

Her father gazed at her. "If only I could guarantee that in writing. It's so hard to let you grow up."

"But I am growing up," she reminded him.

"We sent you to Pennsylvania for sleep-away camp partly so you could make friends outside of Hollywood," he said. "Expand your horizons a little. Like Natalie Goode has done."

"What, so I can talk to them on the internet?" Tori said. She could hear her voice rising, but she couldn't seem to stop herself from sounding upset. She *was* upset.

"Daddy, Natalie lives in Manhattan, not Malibu!"

"Well, we could have her come visit," her dad said. "You said there was going to be a reunion. Maybe we could plan something, too."

"We're talking about Michael," Tori said. "A *boy* who lives *here*."

"James," her mother said, laying a hand on her father's arm. "Let's walk."

As Tori watched, her mother slipped her arm through her father's and they strolled off together.

Just then, someone whispered her name from the bushes.

It was Michael! She darted behind the bush.

"I'm sorry I got you in trouble," Michael said.

"No, I got me in trouble," she said.

She was watching her parents. They were obviously deep in conversation. Then they stopped and faced each other.

Michael said, "I don't know if this is a good time to tell you this, but I felt bad that I asked you to sneak out. But I couldn't figure out what else to do so I could hang out with you."

As rattled as she was, she couldn't help but smile at him. She looked up at him through her sparkly lashes and said, "Ditto here. Exactly."

"Do you want me to talk to your parents for you?" Michael asked.

Tori giggled. "That's sweet, but I'm not sure what good it would do."

"Yeah. You're right. He's the Hollywood lawyer.

There's no way I could beat him at the negotiation game." He sighed. Then he shyly slipped his hand around Tori's. Chills shot up and down her spine. She was holding hands with Michael!

With her fingers laced through his, she stepped out of the bushes and into plain sight. She didn't want there to be any more sneaking around.

Her parents were deep in conversation. Tori could tell her mom was wearing down her dad. Then her dad turned his head and saw her with Michael. She gave him the most imploring look she could muster.

Please, please, please, can I keep him?

Her dad smiled and shook his head.

"He's giving us the 'green light', as they say in the biz." Tori bounced up and down.

"But he's shaking his head," Michael said cautiously.

"I know!" Tori cried. "That just means he's giving up. Which isn't something he's used to doing." Then, as if to prove her point, her father waved them away.

"I guess that's our signal!" Tori exclaimed. And then for the very first time, she wrapped her arms around Michael's torso and gave him a gigantic hug.

EPILOGUE

Posted by: Alyssa
Subject: Thanksgiving!

Hello, campers!

It's me, your official Double-Bunk-Blog T'giving Hostess! We have had a lot of excitement since Halloween. Priya, rock on with your bad self. It's so cool that they are doing an article about your science fair exhibit with Jordan in the school paper.

And I'm sure that everyone's also thrilled to hear that Priya has helped Jordan solve his dilemma about what to buy Miss Brynn, and that she will be receiving it next week, for her b'day! Be sure to tell us what it is, Brynn!

Val, your pix of the recital were awesome!

You killed, grrl! And Tori, way to go with Michael. Sweet pix of you, M & Kallista at Malibu.

Here's a Thanksgiving contest. Write down how many things you are most grateful for in your life today. Longest list wins!

One thing I am grateful for is my artistic talent. *Ode to a Woman* is now hanging in a small gallery downtown – and Natalie's mom is talking to her art gallery about commissioning some work from me! (Check it out! Commissioning! I know the lingo!)

And I am extra grateful for all my wonderful, supportive CLFs, who have stood by me and believed in me! I'm sure I speak for every one of us who has had "exciting challenges" this month! When it comes to looking out for one another, CLFs are the best!

Keep in touch and keep us all up to date on what's going on with you!

TTFN,

Lyss

To: MichaelS
From: Tori
Subject: President's Day Ski Weekend

Dear Michael,

Great news! My dad is totally on board with inviting some of my Camp Lakeview friends out to spend President's Day Weekend skiing with us in Tahoe. But I can only invite five. FIVE! And I have, like TWENTY-five camp girlfriends. I don't know what to do.

XO, Tori

To: Tori
From: MichaelS
Subject: Re: President's Day Ski Weekend

Dear Tori,

I totally get that. I got to invite THREE guys to my dad's location shoot at the Indianapolis 500. It was tough. I'll tell you what worked for me if you think that would help. IM at 8:30?

Tori smiled as she typed back, *YES!*

It was *so* cool to have a boyfriend in the industry! *And* to realize that she had made good friends at Camp Lakeview. Lots of them! So many, in fact, that she was going to have a very hard time deciding whom to invite on the trip.

But whichever five I pick, she thought, *I know we'll have a blast.*

And that was definitely something to put on her list of things she was thankful for.

Turn the page for a sneak
preview of more

SUMMER CAMP
SECRETS

ON THIN ICE

CHAPTER ONE

Posted by: Tori

Subject: Sunny SoCali

Hiya Lakeview gal pals,

It's January and I'm staring out the window at the bright LA sunshine, wishing you were all here with me to enjoy it! Don't hate me, but it's twenty degrees out today. I heard about the big storm that just blew through NJ and NY, so I figured I'd check in with you to make sure you weren't buried under three metres of snow. Believe it or not, I wish I got to see snow more often out here. So, what's new with you guys? Write back ASAP. I miss you all!

Love,

Tori

Tori sighed, took one more glance out the window, and reluctantly fixed her gaze on her computer, where her e-mail was up and running. Her Camp Lakeview friends would say that she was so lucky if they saw this beautiful weather. In truth, Tori felt anything *but* lucky today.

The cursor on the screen blinked at her, waiting, but the words Tori knew she had to write just wouldn't come. She was supposed to be sending out an E-vite for the ski weekend her parents had told her she could have up in Lake Tahoe over Presidents' Day weekend, but instead, she was turning into the Queen of Procrastination.

The list of the five names she'd chosen was sitting next to her keyboard, but the longer she looked at it, the more horrible it seemed. Jenna, Alyssa, Nat, Grace and Sarah – the only girls she was going to invite on the trip. She'd tried to pick the five girls she knew the best from Camp Lakeview, but also the five girls who would match up the best for the long weekend. Nat and Alyssa were inseparable, and Tori'd gotten along great with Jenna, Nat and Grace all summer long. On top of that, Jenna was loads of fun, always pulling pranks and kidding around. And Sarah was Miss Athletic, but not as obsessed about it as Alex, so Tori figured she'd catch on to skiing right away and would be able to help the other girls learn.

Some of the other Lakeview girls wouldn't have worked out nearly as well for the trip. Chelsea, for instance, was a total downer, always whining and bossing everyone else around. Karen was sweet, but she was too quiet. And Priya spent so much time with her best friend, Jordan, that Tori felt uncomfortable asking her to come skiing without him. But what about Brynn? And Valerie? And Alex? Tori wasn't as close to them, but they'd all been nice to her over the summer. And Alex and Jenna were great friends, and so were Brynn and Grace. How could she ask Jenna without asking Alex? Or Grace without Brynn? Every time she thought she'd picked the right five girls, heaps of doubt crowded into her brain. There was no way she could possibly send out this E-vite.

Tori gave her computer one final glare and headed for the gym, where she knew her parents were playing their daily game of squash.

Maybe there was still the teeny, tiniest chance that her parents would change their minds. It was worth one last shot.

Her dad had had the glass-enclosed gym built as a rooftop addition to their house. Tori's parents were into juice bars and fitness, but Tori had only used the gym a handful of times (and that was when she had her friends over for Pilates). When she got to the top of the gym stairs, she found her parents prepping for the sauna.

"How was your game?" Tori asked.

Her mom grinned. "I'm reigning champion."

"And I'm the resident sulker," her dad added.

Tori laughed. "That's okay, Dad. You can still beat me any day."

"Coming from someone who never plays, I'm not sure that's a compliment." Her dad smiled. "And to what do we owe this unexpected visit? You never come up here, sweetie. What's going on?"

Tori took a deep breath and dived right in. "I wanted to talk to you about the ski trip." She turned on her best doe-eyed, pleading daughter face. "Isn't there any way I can invite more of my friends? I know you said only five girls tops, but we can rent another apartment so more can come. I'll even help pay for it with my savings."

Her mom shook her head. "The money in your savings is for college. You know that."

Tori chanced another look at her dad, but he wasn't budging either. "Sweetheart, we've been over this before. Our apartment only sleeps seven comfortably, and two girls are already going to have to share a bed."

"They can bring sleeping bags," Tori started, "and extra pillows. Or sleep on the couch with blankets. The couch is big and—"

Her dad held up his hand before she could say

anything else. "We agreed that we'd pay for the lift tickets, ski rentals and food for five of your friends. I'm sorry, Tori, but the decision's final."

Tori bit her lip. "But I can't choose between my friends like this. It's just not fair."

Her mom kissed her forehead. "Honey, I know it's a tough decision for you, but if your friends are as nice as you say they are, they're going to understand. And tough choices like this are all part of growing up."

"And if all else fails," her dad added, "you can blame this on your evil parents. We'll take the fall."

"It's not that simple," Tori said, but she could see that her parents had made up their minds. She was stuck with their decision, awful as it was. "I'm going to the beach with Michael this afternoon," she said, sighing as she turned away. "I'll have my cellphone if you need me."

Tori had met Michael a few months ago, and for a while, they'd been like a regular Romeo and Juliet. Michael was the son of one of Tori's dad's clients, so at first her dad had forbidden her to date him. Eventually, though, her dad came around, and now Tori could see Michael whenever she wanted, without all the Shakespearean drama (although sneaking around *had* been kind of fun).

But now, even spending the afternoon with him

didn't do anything to improve Tori's mood. She sat in the warm sand, watching Michael skim the waves on his surfboard, but all she could think about was the ski trip. She barely even noticed when Michael sat down next to her, until he nudged her playfully, shaking a few drops of salty water onto her.

"Still zoning out about your friends, huh?" he said.

Tori nodded. "I can't cancel the whole trip just because I can't invite everyone. But the girls I'm not inviting are going to hate me for ever."

"Hey, nobody could hate you." He smiled. "It's just not possible. But maybe your other friends could pay their own way? If they rented an apartment on their own, your parents couldn't say much, could they?"

"No," Tori said, "but that'll never happen. The girls that I'm inviting already have to pay for their plane tickets out here, and that can get pretty pricey. There's no way everyone else could afford plane tickets, food, lift tickets, rentals *and* an apartment. Even if they split it, nobody our age has that kind of money."

"So what are you going to tell the girls you're not inviting?" Michael asked. "I mean, you can't just keep it a secret for the next month, can you?"

A knot the size of a watermelon tightened in Tori's stomach. The thought *had* crossed her mind. A secret wouldn't be as bad as lying, would it? Tori sighed and rubbed her forehead. This whole thing was giving her one massive headache. "I don't know what I'm going to tell them. But no matter what, it won't be fun. We might as well cancel our movie plans for tomorrow, because I'll be busy getting killed by my former friends."

Michael laughed. "There won't be any killing. Yelling, maybe, but no killing."

"Thanks for that vote of confidence," Tori said, laughing a little. "Maybe I'll just change my name and move out of the country if that happens."

"But not before the movie tomorrow," said Michael.

"Not one second before." Tori smiled.

"And in the meantime," Michael said, "how about coming for a little water ride with me?" He nodded to his surfboard.

"The Pacific Ocean in January?" Tori asked. "No thanks. You have a wetsuit. I don't."

"A walk, then?" Michael tried again, holding out his hand.

"Now that I can handle." Tori grinned.

That night, after she'd said goodbye to Michael, Tori sat back down at her computer to fill out the E-vite for the trip. She'd felt better after the beach, but now her heart was pounding with fear all over again. As she started typing, she knew one thing for certain. If making decisions like this was part of "growing up", as her mom had said, then she didn't want any part of it. No way.

"Sarah!" Abby yelled from the bottom of the stairs. "Are you coming sometime in the next millennium, or am I going to have to go to the batting cages without you?"

Sarah giggled as she pulled her light brown hair into a ponytail and grabbed her softball bat and glove from her bedroom closet. Abby could be *soooo* impatient sometimes, especially when sports were involved. Like right now, for example. Even though softball season wouldn't start for another three and a half months, and there was no chance of practising outside in the bitter New England snows they'd been having, Abby insisted that they go to the indoor batting cages every Sunday afternoon to keep from getting rusty.

Sarah stuck her head out the bedroom door and saw Abby pacing at the bottom of the stairs. "I'm almost ready!" she said. "Why don't you come up here for a minute? I promised Alex and Brynn I'd fill them in on my date with David last night." David was the first guy Sarah had ever really liked. In the past, she'd usually wanted to beat up boys instead of hold their hands, but that had changed over the summer when she met David. He lived in Vermont, so she didn't get to see him very often, but his dad had come to Boston on a business trip this weekend and brought David along with him. It had been great to see him, and she couldn't help wanting to spill the details. "How about I check my e-mail superfast right now," Sarah called down to Abby, "and then I'll tell the girls that the date went great, and that I'll fill them in on the whole story later. Deal?"

Abby gave Sarah a very exaggerated frown. "All right," she said finally, climbing the stairs. "As long as I don't have to hear about how he held your hand in the movie theatre for the whole show. You've told me ten times already. And we get to stay at the batting cages for an extra fifteen minutes."

Sarah grinned. "You got it."

Sarah and Abby went to the same middle school in Stowbridge, a tiny town just outside of Boston. Last summer at Lakeview was the first time Sarah had really gotten to know Abby, and even though they'd gotten off to a rocky start, by the end of camp they were great friends.

Sarah knew how important their softball training was to Abby, so she made sure to keep her e-mail to the girls short, promising details later. But just as she was about to disconnect, a new message popped up:

Ski Weekend! You're Invited!

Host: Tori

When: Presidents' Day weekend, February 16–19

Where: Lake Tahoe

It's time to hit the slopes, Lakeview Ladies! My parents have a fab apartment that's right off the lifts at Squaw Valley, and they're footing the bill for food, lift tickets, ski rentals and lessons. All you need to do is buy your plane ticket, and you're set. I can't wait to see you!

Will you attend?   ____Yes   _____No

Sarah practically screamed with excitement, a huge smile spreading across her face. Going skiing with Abby and all the other girls from Camp Lakeview would be such a blast. She'd never been skiing before, and even though she and Abby had thrown around the idea of going up to Vermont for a weekend, she'd heard that East Coast skiing couldn't even come close to West Coast skiing. The West Coast had dibs on sunshiny weather, perfect powder and gorgeous snow-capped mountains. This ski trip had her name written all over it.

"Why do you look like you just won the lottery?" Abby asked, peering at Sarah's ecstatic face.

"Oh, wait till you hear this," Sarah started, ready to share the good news. Abby would be totally psyched, and the two of them could start planning for the trip together.

But just as she was about to read the whole E-vite out loud, a nagging sensation made Sarah skim over the invite list. And there it was, plain as day: Jenna, Alyssa, Nat, Grace and Sarah. No Abby, and no Alex, Brynn, Priya, or Valerie, either. Could that be a mistake? Maybe the E-vite got screwed up and left some of the girls off the list. She'd have to check with Tori. But in the meantime, what was she going to tell Abby?

"Earth to Sarah," Abby said, laughing and waving a hand in front of Sarah's face. "So? What's the big news?"

"Um," Sarah stalled, clicking the E-vite closed and quickly skimming through her other e-mails for another piece of news. There was an e-mail from Nat, and as soon as Sarah read it, she knew it was perfect to share with Abby.

"Guess what?" she said, trying to match the enthusiastic tone she'd had before. "Nat's up in Connecticut right now visiting her cousins, and she's going to see Simon today! She hasn't seen him in a few months."

"That's it?" Abby said, deflated. "*That's* the big news? Yeesh, I thought you were going to tell me something super-exciting."

"Well, it's exciting for Nat," Sarah said, feeling completely stupid. "It's great, you know, that she's getting to see him and everything."

Abby grinned and shook her head. "Yeah, it is. I'm happy for her. But *now* can we go hit some balls?"

"Sure," Sarah said, slipping on her coat and gloves. As they walked to the neighbourhood rec centre, Sarah reminded herself to e-mail Tori to get the scoop on the trip later. She was sure this was all a mix-up, and that Abby and the other girls would be invited as soon as it was all straightened out. But in the meantime, a persistent guilt settled down inside her for a nice, long stay. Not because she was on the E-vite list and Abby wasn't, but because she'd just lied to one of her very best friends for the first time ever. And no matter how many ways she rationalized it, it didn't feel right at all.

To find out what happens next read

On Thin Ice

Out now!

Complete your collection of

SUMMER CAMP SECRETS

Pack the perfect summer accessory
in your beach bag today!

MISS MANHATTAN

City chick Natalie is surprised to find that she actually
enjoys summer camp – until her big secret gets out…
ISBN 9780746084557

PRANKSTER QUEEN

Mischievous Jenna is famous for her wild stunts, but this
year she's totally out of control. What's bugging her?
ISBN 9780746084564

BEST FRIENDS?

Fun-loving Grace starts hanging out with Gaby from rival
bunk 3C, before she realizes what a bully Gaby can be.
ISBN 9780746084571

LITTLE MISS NOT-SO-PERFECT

Sporty, reliable Alex seems like the perfect camper. But
she's hiding a problem that she can't bear to admit.
ISBN 9780746084588

BLOGGING BUDDIES

The girls are back home and keeping in touch through their
camp blog. But one bunkmate needs some extra support.
ISBN 9780746084601

PARTY TIME!

Everyone's excited about the camp reunion in New York! But when it gets to party time, will the girls still get on?
ISBN 9780746084618

THREE'S A CROWD

New camper Tori is from LA and is just as super-hip as Natalie. Good thing Nat isn't the jealous type – or is she?
ISBN 9780746093382

WISH YOU WEREN'T HERE

Sarah stresses when classmate Abby turns up at camp – will she expose Sarah as a geek to all her fun-loving friends?
ISBN 9780746093399

JUST FRIENDS?

Priya's best friend is a boy but she's sure she could never have a crush on him – until he starts to like another girl...
ISBN 9780746093405

JUST MY LUCK

When practical jokes start happening during Colour War, Jenna is the obvious suspect. But could someone else be to blame?
ISBN 9780746093412

FALLING IN LIKE

Valerie's wicked stepsister, Tori's forbidden crush, Alyssa's censored artwork...life back home after camp is so complicated!
ISBN 9780746093429

ON THIN ICE

Tori's only allowed to invite five friends on her fab holiday weekend. But how can she choose without hurting anyone?
ISBN 9780746093436

All priced at £4.99

Fancy some more sizzling Summer Camp fun?

✱ Try out Natalie's favourite magazine quizzes and learn how to draw like Alyssa

✱ Discover Jenna's recipes for the best-ever s'mores and Sarah's hottest tips for the most fun things to do on holiday

✱ Get the lowdown on all the best bits of Camp Lakeview, from the girls' fave games to tried-and-true campfire songs

✱ Plus, look out for fab competitions, and even get the chance to star on the Summer Camp Secrets website yourself!

It's all at

www.summercampsecrets.co.uk

Check it out now!